THE SKY DEVIL

SELECTED FICTION WORKS BY
L. RON HUBBARD

FANTASY
The Case of the Friendly Corpse

Death's Deputy

Fear

The Ghoul

The Indigestible Triton

Slaves of Sleep & The Masters of Sleep

Typewriter in the Sky

The Ultimate Adventure

SCIENCE FICTION
Battlefield Earth

The Conquest of Space

The End Is Not Yet

Final Blackout

The Kilkenny Cats

The Kingslayer

The Mission Earth Dekalogy*

Ole Doc Methuselah

To the Stars

ADVENTURE
The Hell Job series

WESTERN
Buckskin Brigades

Empty Saddles

Guns of Mark Jardine

Hot Lead Payoff

A full list of L. Ron Hubbard's
novellas and short stories is provided at the back.

*Dekalogy—a group of ten volumes

L. RON HUBBARD

THE SKY DEVIL

GALAXY
PRESS

Published by
Galaxy Press, LLC
7051 Hollywood Boulevard, Suite 200
Hollywood, CA 90028

Printed in the United States of America.

ISBN-10 1-59212-401-1
ISBN-13 978-1-59212-401-5

Library of Congress Control Number: 2007903612

Contents

STORIES FROM PULP FICTION'S GOLDEN AGE

AND it *was* a golden age.

The 1930s and 1940s were a vibrant, seminal time for a gigantic audience of eager readers, probably the largest per capita audience of readers in American history. The magazine racks were chock-full of publications with ragged trims, garish cover art, cheap brown pulp paper, low cover prices—and the most excitement you could hold in your hands.

"Pulp" magazines, named for their rough-cut, pulpwood paper, were a vehicle for more amazing tales than Scheherazade could have told in a million and one nights. Set apart from higher-class "slick" magazines, printed on fancy glossy paper with quality artwork and superior production values, the pulps were for the "rest of us," adventure story after adventure story for people who liked to *read*. Pulp fiction authors were no-holds-barred entertainers—real storytellers. They were more interested in a thrilling plot twist, a horrific villain or a white-knuckle adventure than they were in lavish prose or convoluted metaphors.

The sheer volume of tales released during this wondrous golden age remains unmatched in any other period of literary history—hundreds of thousands of published stories in over nine hundred different magazines. Some titles lasted only an issue or two; many magazines succumbed to paper shortages during World War II, while others endured for decades yet. Pulp fiction remains as a treasure trove of stories you can read, stories you can love, stories you can remember. The stories were driven by plot and character, with grand heroes, terrible villains, beautiful damsels (often in distress), diabolical plots, amazing places, breathless romances. The readers wanted to be taken beyond the mundane, to live adventures far removed from their ordinary lives—and the pulps rarely failed to deliver.

In that regard, pulp fiction stands in the tradition of all memorable literature. For as history has shown, good stories are much more than fancy prose. William Shakespeare, Charles Dickens, Jules Verne, Alexandre Dumas—many of the greatest literary figures wrote their fiction for the readers, not simply literary colleagues and academic admirers. And writers for pulp magazines were no exception. These publications reached an audience that dwarfed the circulations of today's short story magazines. Issues of the pulps were scooped up and read by over thirty million avid readers each month.

Because pulp fiction writers were often paid no more than a cent a word, they had to become prolific or starve. They also had to write aggressively. As Richard Kyle, publisher and editor of *Argosy*, the first and most long-lived of the pulps, so pointedly explained: "The pulp magazine writers, the best of them, worked for markets that did not write for critics or attempt to satisfy timid advertisers. Not having to answer to anyone other than their readers, they wrote about human beings on the edges of the unknown, in those new lands the future would explore. They wrote for what we would become, not for what we had already been."

Some of the more lasting names that graced the pulps include H. P. Lovecraft, Edgar Rice Burroughs, Robert E. Howard, Max Brand, Louis L'Amour, Elmore Leonard, Dashiell Hammett, Raymond Chandler, Erle Stanley Gardner, John D. MacDonald, Ray Bradbury, Isaac Asimov, Robert Heinlein—and, of course, L. Ron Hubbard.

In a word, he was among the most prolific and popular writers of the era. He was also the most enduring—hence this series—and certainly among the most legendary. It all began only months after he first tried his hand at fiction, with L. Ron Hubbard tales appearing in *Thrilling Adventures, Argosy, Five-Novels Monthly, Detective Fiction Weekly, Top-Notch, Texas Ranger, War Birds, Western Stories,* even *Romantic Range.* He could write on any subject, in any genre, from jungle explorers to deep-sea divers, from G-men and gangsters, cowboys and flying aces to mountain climbers, hard-boiled detectives and spies. But he really began to shine when he turned his talent to science fiction and fantasy of which he authored nearly fifty novels or novelettes to forever change the shape of those genres.

Following in the tradition of such famed authors as Herman Melville, Mark Twain, Jack London and Ernest Hemingway, Ron Hubbard actually lived adventures that his own characters would have admired—as an ethnologist among primitive tribes, as prospector and engineer in hostile climes, as a captain of vessels on four oceans. He even wrote a series of articles for *Argosy,* called "Hell Job," in which he lived and told of the most dangerous professions a man could put his hand to.

Finally, and just for good measure, he was also an accomplished photographer, artist, filmmaker, musician and educator. But he was first and foremost a *writer,* and that's the L. Ron Hubbard we come to know through the pages of this volume.

This library of Stories from the Golden Age presents the best of L. Ron Hubbard's fiction from the heyday of storytelling, the Golden Age of the pulp magazines. In these eighty volumes, readers are treated to a full banquet of 153 stories, a kaleidoscope of tales representing every imaginable genre: science fiction, fantasy, western, mystery, thriller, horror, even romance—action of all kinds and in all places.

Because the pulps themselves were printed on such inexpensive paper with high acid content, issues were not meant to endure. As the years go by, the original issues of every pulp from *Argosy* through *Zeppelin Stories* continue crumbling into brittle, brown dust. This library preserves the L. Ron Hubbard tales from that era, presented with a distinctive look that brings back the nostalgic flavor of those times.

L. Ron Hubbard's Stories from the Golden Age has something for every taste, every reader. These tales will return you to a time when fiction was good clean entertainment and the most fun a kid could have on a rainy afternoon or the best thing an adult could enjoy after a long day at work.

Pick up a volume, and remember what reading is supposed to be all about. Remember curling up with a *great story.*

—Kevin J. Anderson

KEVIN J. ANDERSON *is the author of more than ninety critically acclaimed works of speculative fiction, including The Saga of Seven Suns, the continuation of the Dune Chronicles with Brian Herbert, and his* New York Times *bestselling novelization of L. Ron Hubbard's* Ai! Pedrito!

THE SKY DEVIL

CHAPTER ONE

ONE notch on a gauge, five gallons of gas, one hour's
flying time. After that, the Sahara—no water, oceans
of shifting sands and no one would either know or care that
Vic Kennedy was dead.

But the one notch, the five gallons, remained, and while
the engine still bellowed and while the plane bored southeast,
Vic Kennedy was content to sit and watch the needle and
the unvarying, never-ending panorama of the desert as it
unfolded, touched by the ship's shadow.

His shoulder was numb and he was pleased about it. Perhaps
it would stay numb until he had to land. It seemed that his
shoulder had hurt forever.

He'd never reach Liberia. He had known that he would
never reach it. But when he had landed the former Greek
premier at Alexandria they had told him to fly on, that the
British could do nothing for a Greek rebel; but a premier—well,
that was different.

And when he had reached Algiers, the French had given
him gas and nothing else, and had told him that he was not
wanted there. They had not even bandaged that nagging
wound under his shoulder.

They had told him that he might find refuge in Liberia,

3

that perhaps he could convince the Liberians that they needed a pilot to train an air corps for them.

The old Greek two-seater was hanging on desperately. Wings riddled, a flying wire gone, a knock in the engine where a bullet had scraped an ignition wire . . .

Vic Kennedy's dark-circled gray eyes stared down at the sand ocean of the Algerian Sahara. His ragged khaki shirt flapped in the whipping slipstream, his artillery-booted feet were curiously heavy on the rudders. His left hand was leaden on the stick.

Well, he thought, it had been a good war after all. Even if he had chosen the wrong side, even if he had volunteered to bring the rebel premier to Alexandria. And now it was all over and over forever. The French didn't want him. The British wouldn't let him stay. And a quick execution was awaiting him back there in Greece.

One notch and then when the gas needle dropped through that, he would have to land and take the punishment the desert meted out. No water, no habitations, nothing but sand.

At least it was growing cooler as the sun settled in its own flame. The bucking heat waves were less persistent. Dusk was already creeping in from the east. Perhaps he had better land and get it over with.

At night you didn't have to watch the mirages dance invitingly along the world's rim—like that one to the south. Mirages were too hard on a man. That one to the south consisted of shimmering mountains, a cool blue expanse of water and a cluster of shining buildings.

But they didn't build mosques in the Sahara and they didn't have lakes and that was that. In a moment the illusion would be gone. Not, of course, that Vic Kennedy gave a damn. It was all over for him.

The sun went down a little more and started to spin and burn. The biplane roared onward almost lost between an expanse of sky and sand.

Vic Kennedy turned his tired eyes toward the mirage again. He might as well look at it anyway.

With something like interest he aroused himself from the lethargy and scrutinized that inviting scene. Certainly it should have faded long before this. Perhaps it was real, after all. And if it was—well, did it matter so much where he died?

He banked and placed the city between the top cylinders of the engine. He wouldn't turn on that five-gallon reserve. Not yet. The needle still showed some in the main tank—perhaps four gallons.

Suspiciously, he cut his gun and nosed down through the blue gloom which was settling across the world. By slipping the plane he could look straight ahead at the buildings. Odd that they stayed right there and didn't move at all. It was some trick of light, naturally, but it was interesting.

The city was apparently built on a steep hillside, and from the air the streets looked like steps going up. A minaret raised its lofty star and crescent into the dusk. A palace sprawled in languid magnificence in the exact center of the town. Flat-roofed houses took on a sturdy appearance—too solid for a mirage.

Vic Kennedy's heart began to pound against his ribs. He caught himself up, told himself that he wouldn't be let in for this old desert trick. The shock of reality would be too great.

But the city persisted in getting larger and even more material. The palace domes glittered in the fading day. And there in the street—Vic made himself look very carefully—a troop of horsemen were moving. Even from a thousand feet, Vic could see that they wore veils.

Tuaregs!

He was almost on the point of shooting the gas to the engine when his eye fell on the gauge. Only four gallons and five in reserve—not enough to go anywhere. But Tuaregs, those desert raiders . . .

When he had been a pilot on the Trans African Air Lines he had found out a great deal about Tuaregs. They were a strange people, living by the sword. He had not known that Tuaregs ever settled in one place, but they evidently did.

A wide parade ground offered itself for a landing field, but Vic Kennedy shied away from it. They hadn't spotted his silent wings as yet and if he could land on the outskirts, unnoticed, he might be able to escape with his life.

Drifting through the twilight, wires sibilant, engine muttering as it idled, he scanned the mountainside for another landing field.

A string of battlements rose above the town, gray and sullen. Towers were square silhouettes against the red haze left by the departed sun. The walls followed the flat ridge of the mountain range.

Kennedy banked and looked down upon the structure. A

flat walk had been built some five hundred feet in length, bordered by low shrubs, bisecting a sprawling garden. In this quiet air it would be quite possible to land there, and the consequences might be better than a try at loose sand.

At least he would not be immediately spotted here. In his preoccupation of studying the walk, he failed to notice the twenty-foot walls which ringed the garden.

The plane sideslipped in, leveled out, and the ground rushed up to meet the reaching wheels. The controls loosened and the ship settled with a crunch to run heavily over the gravel. Shrubs brushed the underside of the bottom wing.

He crawled out of the pit, stiff and weary. His khaki shirt made a crackling sound as he moved his right arm. Blood had caked there, leaving a black, brittle patch along his side.

Taking off his helmet and goggles he laid them upon the seat. His tangled brown hair rippled in the evening breeze. From the garden about him came a dozen pleasing scents. From the town below came the cry of the muezzin calling out the sunset prayer.

The walls which ringed him in were higher than he had anticipated. But then, perhaps, someone would be living here, and if he remembered his Arabic and his Moslem customs, he might be able to impose upon the inhabitant for bed and food. Allah alone knew what a Tuareg would decide.

He went toward the nearest tower, his artillery boots scuffing the stone and crunching over the gravel. He knew he was far from imposing in his torn and dirty khaki, and that, at best, he could expect a beggar's reception.

What he did not know was that his breadth of shoulders,

slenderness of waist and the sturdy handsomeness of his face branded him as a gentleman. And he had forgotten those worthless bands of gold braid on his epaulets and that his boots had been tailored on Savile Row—a fact which not even dust could hide.

The door which opened into the tower swung back on well-oiled hinges. A flight of curving steps went down into the dim interior.

He proceeded slowly, not wanting to surprise a guard into disastrous action. His eyes became accustomed to the dimness and he could see the silk hangings, the soft rugs, and the piles of colored cushions which were strewn about the room. He felt uncomfortably like a burglar.

He saw the girl the instant she saw him. Their eyes met and clashed in mutual surprise. She looked very small and helpless, holding her head out of the silken pillows. Her eyes were wide and round and gray and her full lips were trembling. Two pearl-like tears overflowed and coursed their slow way down her cheeks.

He felt more like a burglar than ever. Uneasily, he broke their gaze and looked for another exit. Finding none he stared back at the girl. She sat up a little straighter and her mouth tightened.

By the change in her expression, he knew that she was about to call for help. In two quick strides he was beside her. She struggled up and he pressed her back.

In the Arabic he had learned long ago, he said: "Do not call. I mean no harm."

"Who are you? What right have you to come here? If my father knew of this, he would kill you."

"Your father?"

"Yes. Troops are outside the gate, on guard. If you are a *jinnī*—"

"A *jinnī*?" He suppressed a smile. It had been long since he had heard that word for evil spirit. The modern Mohammedan had almost forgotten it.

"But no. You can be no *jinnī*." She looked at his wounded shoulder. "A *jinnī* cannot be hurt." She drew away from him. "But how did you get here? This palace is guarded. There are no other entrances but one. My father's troops guard that."

"It matters not how I came here," replied Vic, sinking down on a pillow, aware once more that he was very, very tired. "Are you a prisoner?"

"Why, yes. How did you know?"

"You said that this palace was guarded. Why do they keep you here?"

"Because I threatened to run away into the desert. Quick, you had better go the way you came. They will be coming here soon and if they find you with me, they will kill you. Please go."

"Why did you threaten that?"

"Because I did not want to marry El As'ad." The tears welled up again. "He is ugly and his legs are twisted. But he is the son of Es Samad and my father has ordered me to marry him."

"Who is your father and who are you?"

"You do not know? Surely you must be a stranger to this country. You are certainly an *imajeghen*, perhaps even a knight. And I know you must be *Tārgi*, though you speak strangely. Please go. I do not want them to find you here."

It surprised Kennedy to be mistaken for a Tuareg of the noble class. It was not until he again noticed her gray eyes that he understood. Most of these people had gray or hazel eyes and light skins. They were descendants of the purest Berber stock.

"No," he said. "I am an American."

"An Am . . . Amer— I have never heard of that kingdom. Is it far from here?"

"Very far. But you have not told me your name nor who your father is."

"I am the Lady Dunya and my father is King Zahr of this country. Surely you have heard of him. But please do not speak more. They will come in a moment and they will kill you—and you are too—too graceful a knight to be—"

"But I cannot leave," said Kennedy. "I have no place to go and I am tired and hungry."

"I can do nothing for you. Do not stay. When I tried to run away, my father had me sent here to be held for the marriage, and anyone who even speaks with me besides the guard and my own *imghad* will be killed. My father is very angry."

Kennedy stood up. His arm was hurting again, shooting white lightning through his side. "Send for your *imghad* if you can trust them. I want water and bandage and food. I must have them, for I have come far today. Six hundred miles."

"But—then you must be an *ifrīt* of the *jinn*. Six hundred miles in one day? But a *jinnī* cannot be wounded. How is this?"

"Send for the female slaves."

"Perhaps I should not trust them, but—" She struck a small gong and the clear, trembling note hung long in the room.

The female slaves came and stood before Kennedy, their eyes wide with surprise and fear.

Lady Dunya's small voice was crisp. "Bring me food and water and scents. And, if you love me, say nothing of this to anyone."

They were gone and Kennedy began to tug cautiously at his shirt. The fabric was stuck fast to the wound and when it came free, the ragged gash began to bleed once more.

The water and the food came and with it a black silk tunic and blue veil. Dampening a piece of linen, he bathed the wound, cooling its heat. Winding white cloth tightly about it, he let the girl tie the bandage in place. Then he washed his face and wrists.

As he drew the black silk tunic over his head, he was aware of Dunya's intent gaze.

"What's the matter? Are you afraid the women will tell?"

She shook her head. "I was thinking that you must be a man among men. The bullet which struck you went deep. And yet you can move your arm without wincing. You must indeed be a knight of great fame."

"Of no fame whatever," replied Kennedy, seating himself before a tray of piled sweetmeats and bread and scented water. He felt odd, wearing a black tunic. More important somehow.

11

More at peace with himself. And the blue veil which lay on the couch—that was the sign of nobility. Then even the female slaves had thought— It was infinitely good to be considered a somebody again.

He had no more than tasted the food when a scuffling sound came down the curving stairs. Kennedy stood up, leaning a little forward, his gray eyes bright and watchful.

Chapter Two

A man in a swirling djellaba and blue veil stopped at the entrance to the room. In his hand gleamed a straight two-edged sword, four feet long. His knuckles were white on the hilt.

"Who are you?" spat the officer.

Kennedy stepped forward, easily and naturally. "And who are you to thus address me?"

"I am Captain Taj El Mulook, appointed by El As'ad to watch over his bride-to-be."

Kennedy was within three feet of the man. "I have never heard of either yourself or your master."

The Tuareg raised the two-edged sword. "You lie! By the—"

Kennedy slammed his left fist into the officer's face. The sword never came down. Kennedy caught it by the hilt and jerked it away. The captain slumped back against the wall, his lynx eyes throwing sparks. A dagger held to his left wrist by a leather thong flipped into his palm.

The sword swished and clanged as its point threw fire from the stone. The captain straightened, clawing at the blade which was imbedded in his throat. The steel came free and the Tuareg slumped, little by little, to the floor.

Kennedy turned to Dunya. "They will come to see what has happened to this man. Is there another exit?"

13

"None."

He thought of his ship and its small supply of gasoline. He could get out of here, yes, but suddenly he experienced a wave of reluctance at leaving this girl. She was more beautiful than any woman he had ever seen before. And besides, hadn't she tried to help him?

He walked to the top of the steps and called out, "Guard!"

The outer gate creaked as it was thrown back. Men in white veils came through, running, ancient rifles flung across the crooks of their arms. They slowed when they saw Kennedy and then stopped as they realized he should not, could not, be there.

Kennedy's tones were authoritative. "Send immediately for King Zahr. Tell him that I am here."

A man in the lead blinked and stepped slowly back. "But who are you? How did you get here?"

"Tell King Zahr that I am El Kennedy, Abd El Kennedy."

"Shoot him! Zahr will kill us if we—"

Kennedy ducked back into the shelter of the door. A flintlock crashed and the slug yowled away from the wall. Slamming and bolting the door behind him, Kennedy walked down the stairs, unhurried in spite of the hammering on the wood behind him.

Lady Dunya's head was erect and proud. "It is written," she said, "that you were to come too late. Now they will execute you and I will marry El As'ad."

"It is not written that way," said Kennedy. He listened for a moment to the pounding gun butts. Well, he supposed he had asked for it as usual. There was no peace on this earth

14

for him, never anymore, no matter how far he searched. He felt the weariness creeping over him once more.

He sank down on the cushions, trying to think of some way out of this. He was startled when he found that the girl was standing beside him. She ran her slender white fingers through his hair, smoothing it.

The hammering stopped. Time drifted. Dunya took a coal of fire from a copper vessel and lighted the copper lamp on the wall. It cast her slim shadow against the silken draperies.

Footsteps sounded outside and then a sword hilt rapped on the door. "That is Zahr," said Kennedy. "Nothing to do but let him in."

"But he'll kill us! Both of us!"

Kennedy went up the steps and unbarred the entrance. A towering man confronted him, blue-veiled and cloaked in silk. A stone glittered in his turban.

This, Kennedy knew, was Zahr. Soldiers followed the man into the room, to stand against the walls with swords ready. Kennedy turned and faced the king.

"You are an *ifrīt* of the *jinn*," roared Zahr. "Otherwise you could not have gotten here. It will do you no good to try your tricks. You cannot escape. I hold the seal of Solomon!"

Kennedy smiled. "Perhaps I am not a *jinnī*, what then?"

"Then you will receive the penalty. You have disgraced me and the name of my house by visiting my daughter before her wedding day."

Kennedy listened to the rumbling, deep voice and thought of the Atlantic surf rolling up on the shore.

"But," said Zahr in sudden determination, "you must be a *jinni*. How else could you mount these walls?"

Another man was coming down the steps. He limped and when he turned his face to the light, Kennedy saw the uneven teeth, the thin jaw, the sallow complexion, of El As'ad.

El As'ad's voice was quavery, somehow thick and evil. "But he must be a *jinni*. See, he has killed the valiant Taj El Mulook! He has disgraced me as well as yourself, King Zahr."

Dunya turned from As'ad to her father. "But he cannot be a *jinni*. He is a famous knight, that I know. He is wounded and it is impossible to wound a *jinni*. This man is human."

"Wounded?" said Zahr.

"Then if he is wounded he is human!" cried El As'ad. "And I demand that he be burned!"

Kennedy was a little dazed by the unreality of all this. Men arguing whether or not he was a devil. Men who were flanked by sharp swords and strong soldiers.

"Wait," said Kennedy, with a feeling of relief, "I will settle this. As the Lady Dunya says, I am a knight and I am human. But before you entertain thoughts of burning me, perhaps you would like to know that my prowess might be greater than you think."

"You dare boast to me?" cried Zahr.

"I do," said Kennedy. "And I will make good my boasts. How many men have you under arms?"

"A thousand horsemen of the first rank," thundered Zahr. "And a thousand foot soldiers and squires."

"It is scarcely enough for me to bother with," replied

Kennedy with haughtiness. "But I have seen your parade ground beside the palace. On that field, tomorrow morning, I shall vanquish your entire host. They can close in upon me from all four sides and they shall not touch me."

"What is this?" roared Zahr.

"Place them where you please, arm them with their best swords, and let them charge me. If you kill me, then no one will know that I have disgraced your house or ruined the name of your Lady Dunya. If I am victorious you must give me anything I want."

"You bargain with my honor, Zahr? Beware the rage and legions of Es Samad!" shrieked El As'ad.

"Quiet!" said Zahr. "You need not again threaten me with King Es Samad's wrath. And you need have no fear of this man and your honor. He is plainly mad."

"I am not crazy," said Kennedy. "Do this even if only to give yourself amusement."

Zahr walked restlessly back to the entrance, turned and paced the floor. Finally he stopped. "We cannot execute him. To do this we would have to publicly state his crime. And that would mean disgrace for all of us. I think it is best. Yes, I think it is best, mad, sane or a *jinnī*. I will take the Lady Dunya back to my palace and we shall leave this young man here, in these guarded walls."

For a moment Kennedy was afraid El As'ad would remember that if the stranger had entered unobserved he could certainly get out in the same manner. But the men strode from the room, leaving him alone.

Lady Dunya paused for an instant and looked back at Kennedy. There was something in her glance, something in the way she held her head . . .

Kennedy sank down upon the cushions and began to worry about the plane. Maybe that war-torn motor wouldn't start. Maybe the remaining flying wires would snap. Maybe— But he was too tired to worry. With the face of Lady Dunya dancing before him, he slept.

Chapter Three

I N the inky hours before dawn, Kennedy went into the garden. The desert chill was heightened here in the mountains and the breeze was sharp through the black tunic. He wrapped the blue veil about his head and shoulders.

The plane had escaped notice in the excitement and it stood untouched where he had left it. Kennedy's arm was stiff, but he somehow contrived to lift the tail of the ship and wheel it to the far end of the runway. The engine would be loud, but that couldn't be helped.

Pumping gas into each cylinder by turning the prop, he primed the engine. With one mighty yank he jerked the club through. With a protesting cough the engine started, shattering the stillness.

Kennedy slid into the pit and eased the throttle. The chuckling mutter of the warming engine could be heard far, he thought. Rather than go through the nerve-shattering process of sitting and waiting, he decided to risk a cold takeoff.

He could barely see the tower's outline against the sky before him. Ramming the throttle home, he jerked up the tail. The gravel crunched. The wheels went light. With a pulsating snarl, the plane was in the air, flying free. A cylinder missed. The tower loomed before the sagging plane. The motor caught, barked and Kennedy banked sharply. He could see the land below quite plainly in the starlight. He immediately shut off the engine and banked toward the parade ground.

On whispering wings he sailed over the domes of the sleeping palace and lit featherlike upon the hard-packed plain. Evidently no one had seen him come. Feeling accountably pleased with himself, he sank back in the cockpit and dozed.

He awoke with the hot morning sun in his face, awoke with a thunderous murmur of voices ringing in his ears. For a moment he forgot where he was. Forgot that this was no longer Greece and that the attack on Salonika had failed. Forgot that these men were Tuaregs of some lost, hidden kingdom deep in the Sahara. His hands went up to the machine-gun butts and the loading handle was cocked before he came fully awake.

A waving forest of shining metal engulfed him. Faces and veils. Flashing hoofs. Rippling tunics. Mounted on a black charger, Zahr was approaching in the midst of a gleaming array of courtiers.

Kennedy stood up in the pit, waiting. His goggles flashed in the sunlight and the helmet almost obscured his face. Zahr halted, staring with disbelief.

"*Jinnī! Ifrīt!* Marid!" rolled out of a thousand throats.

Kennedy realized, then, that they had never before seen helmets and goggles. He ripped them off and replaced them with the whipping veil, carrying out his role of knight.

Zahr, breathing easier, cantered up. "You are ready?"

"I am ready," replied Kennedy.

"But what is this thing you have here?" demanded Zahr.

"My charger."

"A thing of wood and linen?" cried Zahr. He glanced about him at his men and shook his head. "You should have a care, Abd El Kennedy. When my men charge, they have orders to spit you where you are. They shall show you no mercy."

"Perhaps I shall kill some of them," replied Kennedy. "What then?"

"If you cannot, I shall think you a weakling."

"Then let your troops withdraw from me five hundred paces and allow me to prepare myself."

The face of Lady Dunya was visible for a moment in the crowd. Tuareg women are never veiled, and the beauty of her face, the confidence in her eyes, made Kennedy feel better than he had for months.

The troops were withdrawing. Kennedy dropped to the ground and started his engine. The roar was lost in the rumble of sound about him. People were curious, but not frightened. They kept far back.

"Now," said Kennedy to himself, "if the crate will hold together for a few minutes everything will be all right."

Kennedy raised his hand in salute when the engine had warmed. Zahr's arm went up. A curved horn loosed a thunderous blast.

Drawn in a circle five hundred paces in radius, the columns of cavalry and foot soldiers began to move. The sun flamed from their swords and lances. Djellabas fluttering, veils whipping, the desert raiders plunged forward.

Kennedy jammed the throttle into the dash. The quivering

ship, blasting a gale of dust behind it, crept forward. Pounding hoofs drowned the engine's bellow. The crouched riders flashed nearer on either side.

The tail came off and the plane whipped forward. Kennedy held his breath. He wasn't going to make it. He'd crash into the first rank ahead and splinter his prop. He couldn't lift it off. Where was the wind he had carefully located?

Yanking the sluggish stick back and forward, Kennedy tried to wish the plane off the ground. But the wind wasn't there and the controls were appallingly loose. He could see the bits and curbs of the horses through the top cylinders. He could see the rolling cloud of dust beating through the wings.

They wouldn't veer ahead. They didn't know what they faced and they were unafraid. The king's *mamelukes* were sturdy men. Kennedy clutched on the last resort, his machine guns.

Kicking the rudders right and left, he slammed down on the trip. Glinting brass shells rolled back. The flame was white in the sunlight. Horses and men went down, skidding in the dust, a tangled mass of kicking hoofs and snarled djellabas.

Like a fan, the flanking cavalry spread away from the ship's path. The wheels bumped, came off and Kennedy slashed through the dust of the carnage he had created.

The ship rose steadily toward the peaks; he banked and came back thundering at the crowd of men who milled on the parade ground. Shrieking, they scattered away.

Kennedy zoomed and returned, diving down upon Zahr

himself. He could almost see Zahr's face go white. The black charger reared and pawed air in fright.

In a wingover, Kennedy studied the field. He nodded with satisfaction. They were frightened enough, those people. They were as witless now as they had been determined.

Kennedy slid in for a landing on the clear side of the parade ground. He cut his engine off and rolled toward the spot where Zahr's horse still plunged.

Unfastening his helmet strap, Kennedy climbed out and strode toward the king. A swirl of dust detached itself from the crowd and ran toward him. He stopped. It was Dunya.

It was easy to see that she had not been frightened. She had faith in him, certainly, and from her sparkling eyes, it was more than faith.

Together they approached Zahr, who was quieting his horse and assembling the courtiers, who had come sheepishly from the edges of the field.

The instant he saw Zahr's face, Kennedy knew that he had made a mistake in not remaining in his ship. A mounted man has some intangible advantage over one on foot and Zahr needed every advantage he could muster.

El As'ad's whining voice was behind Zahr. "You see, king of kings? He is a *jinnī*. He soars into the clouds at the slightest pretext. And as he is a *jinnī*, pretending to be human and wounded, you are not bound by any of your oaths. So hath decreed our lord Solomon."

"Quiet," bellowed Zahr, catching sight of Kennedy. "Ho, young man, so you are not a man at all, but a *jinnī*!"

23

Kennedy zoomed and returned, diving down upon Zahr himself.
He could almost see Zahr's face go white.

"Because I routed your troops, I'm an evil spirit?"

Dunya's glance was scornful. "Because he makes good his boast, you would kill him?"

El As'ad's voice was oily behind Zahr. "You need not keep your vow. He belongs to the realm of the *ifrīt*."

Kennedy's mouth was drawn down in a bitter line. "That is the way of cowards, Zahr."

"You call me a coward?"

"What else can I think? You disown your oaths given in faith to me."

El As'ad's whine was insistent. "You would linger long in hell for allowing your daughter to marry a *jinnī*."

"This El As'ad," said Kennedy, "seems to have a great deal of wisdom and advice. If he is great and worthy of your daughter, let him meet me out in the field and we shall see who comes off best."

El As'ad's squinted eyes took in the crumpled clots on the field which had been *mamelukes* and horses. He paled and twisted uneasily on his horse.

"I cannot," said Zahr, "ask him to meet one of the evil region in single combat. I am tied to you neither by vows nor by family. You have not so much as announced yourself my guest. Therefore, because you employ the stratagems of Satan against me and my men, I shall be forced to condemn you to be burned."

Kennedy, looking up at the veiled face, took a desperate plunge. "I can quote more Koran than yourself. You accuse me of being an unbeliever when you yourself are showing me that you know not the value of a vow. King Zahr, I say it to your face that you and El As'ad are cowards, that you know me to be human but that you are afraid of me."

Zahr quivered. He raised his four-foot sword as though to strike. And then when Kennedy failed to flinch, he swept out his arm in a commanding gesture.

"Take him to the palace!" bawled Zahr. "Hold him under heavy guard. Today we shall prepare the wedding festival and tomorrow we shall celebrate by burning this devil."

Hands fastened on Kennedy. He looked at the fearful faces of those about him and shook loose their holds. Slowly he walked in their midst toward the sprawling palace at the side of the lake.

Chapter Four

VIC KENNEDY stretched out on the divan and shifted his right arm into a more comfortable position. It was aching again, damnably. He spent a few moments silently thinking of all the gruesome things he would like to do to the machine-gun battery which had splintered his plane and then wounded him. Those Greek federals had received quite a little punishment, but not nearly enough to suit Kennedy.

But all that seemed far away from him as though he had heard someone tell of it or had seen it on the screen. Had the pilot in that scrap really been Vic Kennedy? His own identity became more intangible to him the more he thought about it. All animosity for the machine gunners had faded.

The patterned ceiling over his head dipped and curved in innumerable arches. Figures were painted there, but he could not quite make them out. He felt that the solving of the paintings would somehow help him now.

Forgetting momentarily the verdict which had recently been passed upon him, he felt at ease. All those turbulent forces which had guided his footsteps in the past months were curiously remote. He knew that he had somehow achieved that thing most desired by so many men: he had succeeded in running away from himself.

Clothed in the black silk tunic, lying among sweet-scented

pillows, he was no longer Captain Victor Kennedy; he was Abd El Kennedy, a nobleman from some far-off place not even he could name.

The incongruity of his thoughts struck him. Here he was, waiting for tomorrow and flame, feeling at ease with himself. He had severed all connections with a world he had come to despise. He had known a beautiful woman, however briefly.

"Perhaps," he murmured, "perhaps it's worth it."

He could have escaped in his ship that morning. It would have been simple. But he would have faced the fate he had avoided not twenty-four hours before. Yes, being burned as a devil was intensely preferable to dying alone in a sand ocean.

Queer that they had quartered him so well in the palace. The food was good and he could at least drink all the water he wanted. The thought of water and the parched Sahara made him thirsty. He rolled over on his side, intending to drink from the copper vessel by the couch. His hand stopped halfway to the tray.

The Lady Dunya was quietly seated beside him, staring at him with strangely intense gray eyes.

"You should not come here," said Kennedy.

"What difference does anything make?"

"But I am a prisoner and no one is supposed to see me. Much less yourself."

She shook her head. "Those were my father's orders, but the *mamelukes* at the door know me and hesitate to disobey my own commands. I found it too hard to stay away."

"If they know you, then would they let me out of here?"

"No. But they would let me in."

"I asked without reason," said Kennedy. "I have no place to go."

"Would your bird carry you where you would?"

"No. It will not fly far, ever again."

"But there are other kingdoms to the south. Several of them. Perhaps you could—"

"They know nothing of me and they would doubtless kill me on sight. Tell me, Dunya, is the bird still on the parade ground?"

"Yes. They fear to touch it. But I am not afraid of it, if it is your servant."

"It is," said Kennedy, unaccountably pleased that she was not afraid of the ship.

"Perhaps if you could get free and reach the bird—"

"No. The—" Arabic for *gasoline* was not in his vocabulary. In fact, there is no word for it. He let the sentence hang. "Tell me of El As'ad. Is he angered with you?"

"No. He dares not be angry—until after we are married. Then—"

Kennedy sat up, scowling in thought. "Certainly there is something that you can do so that he would not marry you."

"He is not thinking of me. He is thinking of an alliance between the kingdoms of Zahr and his father. When I am taken to El As'ad's home, the days of my freedom will be at an end. After that I shall have to face blank walls. I . . . I should have been born a man, El Kennedy."

"No. I utterly disagree with you."

"But to have my wedding day celebrated by the killing of the man I love—"

"But why," Kennedy demanded, "must you marry at all? You say an alliance, but from what I have seen of Zahr, I think he is the wrong type of man to want El As'ad for a prince of his kingdom. Is he blind?"

The Lady Dunya shook her head slowly. "No. You do not understand. Nor did I until my father explained it to me. I know that I really should marry El As'ad for the good of the people."

"How could El As'ad do your people any good as a crown prince?"

Dunya sighed. "That I do not know, El Kennedy. But El As'ad is the son of Es Samad, king of Hamra, far to the south. Hamra was once part of my father's kingdom, but Es Samad revolted and became very powerful.

"Understand, El Kennedy, that my father is not afraid of Es Samad, but he knows that war with the kingdom of Hamra would be disastrous for our people. Therefore, Zahr is forced to accept Es Samad's terms and he must marry me to El As'ad to form an alliance and thus prevent war."

Kennedy frowned. "But I fail to see how that would prevent war. After you are married to El As'ad he becomes a crown prince of this kingdom and in event of Zahr's death, Es Samad would rule both even without a war."

"But," replied Dunya, "if I do not gracefully consent to marry El As'ad, he would steal me from Zahr and I would become a slave in Hamra, thus disgracing the house of Zahr. I can do nothing nor can you. I see now that this is written."

Kennedy leaned back and was silent for a long time. He looked at Dunya calculatingly, measuring her capabilities as coldly as he could.

At last he sat forward. "Dunya, you are not afraid of the bird?"

"No, El Kennedy."

"And if I should tell you of certain parts of the bird, do you think you could do something for me?"

"Yes."

"Then listen. In front there is a thing which spins. Behind that are several black shapes about so big." He cupped his hands, demonstrating the thickness of a cylinder. "And just behind those you will find a small object of brass no thicker than your finger. On one side of this there is a handle which can be easily turned. And when this small brass handle is turned, a white fluid will run out. Do you understand?"

"Yes, El Kennedy."

"Fine. Now, if you would take a copper bucket with you, you could fill it with this fluid and bring it back here to me. Do you think you could do that, Dunya?"

"I can only try."

"But remember this. After you have filled the bucket, turn the handle again until the fluid no longer runs. If you can bring this to me tonight, perhaps—"

The door was flung open and the towering body of Zahr was in the entrance. The eyes above his veil were hard with anger. Behind him, peering under his arm, was El As'ad.

"I thought I would find you here!" roared Zahr. "Did I not forbid you to see this *jinni*? Do you wish to bring destruction down upon my house?"

31

Dunya stood up, edging closer to Kennedy.

El As'ad whined, "He will steal her soul and send to me an *ifrīt* in her body."

Zahr strode across the room and came to a haughty stop before Kennedy. Kennedy stood up and saw that two *mamelukes* had followed Zahr into the room.

"I should kill you now," thundered Zahr. "And I should kill this worthless woman with you. And I would were it not for the execution planned in the morning."

"You do not kill me because you are afraid," replied Kennedy.

Zahr reached out and caught Kennedy's shoulder. The wound sent a livid flash down Kennedy's side. Without thinking he drove out with his left palm. Zahr rocked on his feet. A scarlet splotch appeared on his jaw. He tottered back shaking with rage.

The *mamelukes* jumped forward, swords shimmering. The blades swooped up to strike. Kennedy tried to dodge but he was attacked from either side.

Something swirled in front of him. It was Dunya, throwing out her hands to cover his chest. The *mamelukes* halted the blows.

Lady Dunya's clear voice was calm and commanding. "Go, cattle who call yourselves men."

Zahr stared at her, evidently unable to believe what he had heard. El As'ad's shrill whine was loud and grating. "He has already taken her for a *jinnī*. She is bewitched! This is your making, Zahr. Remember Es Samad's legions!"

Kennedy gently placed Dunya to one side and then stood up to Zahr. "I have said that you were a coward. Perhaps I was wrong in that. Perhaps you know of a *jinnī*'s powers. Perhaps you understand that a *jinnī* could sweep your entire kingdom away with one blow."

Zahr's thin nostrils flared. "I have powers that will prevent that. I am one of the faithful. I have a charm of Solomon which will keep you from causing any harm or playing your tricks."

"Then, if you have a seal, you should not be afraid of me. You know that this seal will keep a *jinnī* from doing anything you do not wish him to do?"

"That I know positively," cried Zahr.

Kennedy smiled. "Then I have the solution to all this. If I were a human being, perhaps you and I could be friends."

"Perhaps," replied Zahr, softening a little.

"And if I am a *jinnī* I cannot use my magic against you."

"That is correct."

"Therefore, if I can show my power with your seal in plain sight, I am a human being."

"You are right," said Zahr.

"We shall understand each other tomorrow."

Zahr and the *mamelukes* strode out, taking Dunya. El As'ad remained glowering an instant in the door, but when he found that he was alone, he scurried away.

Kennedy sank back on the couch. If he could show Zahr in the morning— But there were so many things that might go wrong. So many small details which might crop up and wreck him. And he had to wait until the end was upon him before he could act.

Lying back he resumed his study of the ceiling, but his

peace was blasted. El As'ad's greed, Es Samad's threats. Even if he squared himself with Zahr, he would still have to cope with the kingdom of Hamra. His own freedom would mean nothing. In all this world, was there no peace for a man?

All the rest of the world had faded away from him and he was living in Zahr's kingdom, living in hard reality.

Chapter Five

THE room was cold with a brittle chill. Vic Kennedy shivered as he looked through the narrow arched window at the unruffled lake surface, tinted rose by the coming sun. The palace was still and ghostly, ringed by stringy mist which wafted up from the water. In a few hours they would lead him out to the field. He visualized El As'ad's exultant face.

Kennedy went to the door and listened with his ear to the panel. No sound there. Why hadn't Dunya come with the gasoline?

Had they shut her up in the palace on the hill? Or had she been unable to solve the mystery of the engine petcock? Through the dragging night he had waited anxiously for her footsteps.

It was cold reality now and he wanted to live. This was no longer a toy kingdom. It was peopled with men and surrounded by the steel bonds of greed and revenge and the scrambling search for power. It was a miniature of the world he had known and though he might have found refuge in it, the bitter knowledge of its dangers had brought a returning hardness to Kennedy's face.

More than anything else he wanted to humble El As'ad and show Zahr that even a king can be wrong. That is, he wanted to dwell here as a power and not a captive.

35

With Dunya at his side—but perhaps she, too, had come to think of him as a member of the *ifrīt* clans. Why hadn't she come? Would he have to face the crowd alone?

Fool that he was, he should have stayed in the ship and let Zahr come to him. And if he had not liked Zahr's words he could have blasted his way free, could have hammered them with steel-jacketed lead and made them submit to him.

But then, after all, did he want suspicion and hate around him? The leaders of the Greek rebels had been suspicious of each other. They had tried to acquire their power by treachery and treason. And their revolt had been built on the quicksand of distrust which had ultimately swallowed them.

Now, if he could only show these people that he was a human being after all. Coming to a stop in the center of the room he laughed aloud. That he was a human being. So-called civilization had left witches a hundred years behind and yet he had come to a last stand of superstition.

Aside from their belief in the supernatural, these people were as civilized as any he had ever seen. Descendants of Berbers, white, graceful and intelligent, they appealed to him. And he was no different than any of them. Except for a little advanced knowledge in science which he would be glad to forget.

Damn it, why didn't Dunya come to him?

The artillery boots went down the rug and came back to the door. Once more, for the hundredth time, Kennedy placed his ear to the panel and listened. He relaxed and began to smile.

He stepped back and the door opened. The scowling face

of a *mameluke* stared briefly at him and then Dunya came in. She carried the bucket in her hand.

"All night long," she whispered, "I tried to get away and then the dawn began to come before I could get away from the bird. I thought I would be too late."

Kennedy gripped her arm, shook it gently. Then he took the full copper pail from her. Looking about him he saw a tall vase. He poured the gasoline into it and then upended the bucket.

"Something sharp," he requested.

A glittering pin held her swirling gown across her breast. She unfastened it, holding the cloth tightly in place.

Kennedy tested the point and then punched holes in the bottom of the pail until he could lift out a section of the copper.

"A piece of cloth," he said.

She turned from him and ripped a silk undergarment, handing the ragged blue fragment to him. While she replaced the brooch, he thrust the wadded cloth into the hole and surveyed the job with satisfaction.

"That ought to do the trick," he said in English.

Although she did not understand him, she smiled. "I must go before they start looking for me." She touched his shoulder, looked up into his face and departed.

Kennedy filled up the bucket again, set it beside the door and went back to the couch. He felt a little better although he was aware of a tingling sensation in his throat. He always felt that way before he went into action of any kind, but it seemed to be worse now.

Perhaps it was because he had so much at stake. Never before had he counted anything riches unless he could see the yellow glint. Not that he was particularly mercenary but, like a few million men, he had always had the idea that gold meant everything.

And since he had been here he had not seen one single coin nor had he heard the mention of money. His slant had changed in that he counted his gain in terms of position and freedom. And more than that. Peacefulness and the right to live without care.

An hour passed before a guard of foot soldiers came for him. Two of them were Sudanese, towers of ebony, whose black, shiny nakedness was more striking than clothes ever could have been.

Through their belts, scimitars were thrust. Without waiting for orders or for Kennedy to stand they snatched his arms and jerked him toward the door.

Kennedy stared wildly at the bucket and tried to shake himself free. They were hurting his arm, damn them, and if he failed to get that gasoline . . .

The Sudanese bore him onward, without letting his feet touch the ground. Their polished thick faces were set straight ahead, and the king's *mamelukes* walked in a hollow square, eyes forward.

A low mutter developed outside the palace, growing in volume as they neared the open air. It was a blurred, pulsating sound rolling out of thousands of throats. The Sudanese stopped at the top of the outer steps and set Kennedy down.

He felt humiliated. They had borne him as lightly as though he had been a rubber balloon instead of six feet of brawn.

When the crowd saw him, the roar was stilled. A motionless carpet of faces stretched limitless before him. Unveiled women. Veiled men. Djellabas moving in the wind. Cavalry drawn up in ranks, shields raised, swords glittering.

Once more the mutter began, grew in volume, and then drowned him with sound. The Sudanese gripped his arms and pulled him down the steps to the pavement. The people fell away, leaving a lane for the squad's passage.

Kennedy thought of the gasoline and sighed to himself. It wasn't any use now. Everything would go off on schedule and that would be the end of him.

The parade ground was overflowing with color and faces. A cleared space ended against a solid bank of horsemen who stood silent and motionless. Kennedy's trained eye estimated their number at five hundred. They seemed to be different from the men who had charged the plane the day before. They wore darker cloaks and heavier, longer veils.

Kennedy looked at the opposite end of the field and saw his ship. The people were giving it a wide berth, though many were staring curiously, half fearfully at it.

Straight across from them Kennedy saw Zahr. A platform had been constructed with steps up the front. Pennons fluttered from staffs and draperies rustled in the wind. Zahr was seated upon a carved chair, surrounded by his courtiers.

The Sudanese and the *mamelukes* led Kennedy to the platform. Fifty feet from it, Kennedy saw the pile of splintery kindling and heavy logs. The pyre was square with a hollow center.

Many times in his flying career, Kennedy had seen "roasters," had tried to drag pilots from flaming crates on the chance that they were still alive. He could almost smell the sickening odor of burning flesh.

The steps were under his feet and Zahr's eyes were upon him, imperious and cold. The Sudanese drew their scimitars and stepped back. Kennedy looked behind Zahr and saw El As'ad's uneven teeth displayed in a twisted smile.

CHAPTER SIX

ZAHR held up a lead disc on which characters were engraved. "This is the seal of Solomon. Beware, *jinnī*."

In English, Kennedy said, "To hell with that!" Then he curbed his bubbling anger and replied in Arabic. "I see many strange horsemen here today." Anything for a little time. He had to see Dunya before—

"They are my troops," shrilled El As'ad. "So take care lest your fate be worse than fire."

"Why should you bring your troops?" demanded Kennedy.

"This," said El As'ad with a triumphant smile, "is my wedding day."

Kennedy glanced around him, trying to locate Dunya. "It looks more like a war. Perhaps after you marry Lady Dunya, it will be war."

"What is the meaning of that?" cried Zahr.

"I know that Lady Dunya's hand is the price of peace. It is the one way you can avoid war."

El As'ad stepped away from the king, glaring at Kennedy. "Mind your tongue, *ifrīt* of the *jinn*!"

Zahr's glance had dropped. He lifted his head, tiredly. "I gave El As'ad permission to bring his troops to see his wedding. There is no harm in their seeing your own execution as well."

"I suppose," said Kennedy, "that El As'ad wants this lake and the palace and all your green valleys—rare enough on the Ahaggar Plateau." He knew he was deliberately stirring up a hornets' nest, but he had to have time, time to see Dunya if only for an instant before—

"Quiet!" cried El As'ad. "I forbid your speaking again."

"Do you?" replied Kennedy, his expression as cold and waxen as a marble statue. "Then you do not want Zahr to know how easy it will all be?"

"What do you mean?" snapped Zahr.

"Why," said Kennedy, "it's all simple enough. El As'ad marries the Lady Dunya. That makes him a prince of your kingdom and heir to your throne. It is easier than waging a costly war."

"Quiet!" screamed El As'ad, quivering with anger.

"I'll speak as long as I care to speak," replied Kennedy. "Zahr, I am no prophet, but I know as surely as though I could read the stars that after this marriage you will fall mysteriously ill and die. El As'ad will take your place and join this kingdom to his father's. And you, Zahr, will have lost what you treasure most, your life and your kingdom.

"You are marrying the Lady Dunya to this miscreant, thinking to avoid a disastrous war. It is better to die fighting than by an assassin's poison."

Zahr glanced narrowly at El As'ad and then at Kennedy. "*Jinnī* or not, perhaps you speak words of wisdom. And after we burn you, perhaps I shall forbid this marriage."

Kennedy smiled as he saw the expression on El As'ad's face.

42

El As'ad's voice rose up and broke under the fury of his rage. "You would break your vow? Es Samad and all the troops of Hamra will engulf you!"

"No matter about my daughter. *Mamelukes*, take this *jinnī* to the pyre and apply the flame!"

The Sudanese snatched Kennedy's arms. The rumble of the crowd died to an expectant murmur. Kennedy took one last look about him for Dunya and then allowed himself to be taken.

But before they had gone down three steps, the crowd parted and Dunya ran forward, calling out, "El Kennedy!"

Kennedy stopped and, seeing their princess, the *mamelukes* waited.

Dunya, breathless, her face flushed, lifted the copper bucket from her side and thrust it into Kennedy's hand. "I went back to find you but you had gone. Is this—?"

"Have faith in me," whispered Kennedy.

Zahr's voice thundered down upon them. "Away from him, Dunya! El Kennedy, what is there in that bucket?"

Kennedy turned half about. "Holy water, to assuage the heat of Hell."

"Take him along," roared Zahr.

Kennedy reached down and pulled the cloth out of the bottom. As he went willingly enough, the Sudanese let him walk.

When they reached the pyre, they lifted Kennedy up and dropped him into the center of the square. One of the Sudanese took the bucket from him and proceeded to tie his hands and feet.

Standing there, Kennedy found that the piled wood reached his waist. *Mamelukes* with burning torches in their hands stood by, waiting to apply the flame.

The crowd fell silent. Zahr held up the leaden seal which would hold him safe by nullifying the power of the *jinn*.

"Apply the fire!" bellowed Zahr.

The *mameluke* in front of Kennedy stepped close with his sputtering, spark-throwing torch. He shoved the flame gingerly ahead of him toward the pyre.

But before the torch could reach its destination, an ember fell upon the puddle of gasoline about the bucket. Red tongues sprang up and the soldier leaped back with a startled gasp. He had never before seen water burn.

The three other *mamelukes* stopped, also staring. Flames sprang along the ground, racing before the wind. The crowd did not see the soggy black trail which led from the pyre to the platform. They did not remember that the stream had come from the hole in the bottom of the bucket.

They only saw fire!

Fire racing towards their king!

The wood in front of Kennedy flickered where the gasoline had dripped from Kennedy's soaked boot. His voice was loud in the dead hush of the crowd.

"Fire!" bawled Kennedy. "As a human being, proof against the seal of Solomon as is no *jinnī*, I order you to leap up and devour Zahr!"

The flame raced on along the black trail. It reached the lower step, jumped to the next, crackling.

Kennedy cried out: "Zahr! Do you give me full pardon? Do you admit me to be human?"

Zahr, raised half out of his chair, staring at the red tongues which were coming rapidly nearer, managed to find his voice. The third step from the bottom was blazing, then the next and the next.

Zahr screamed: "Save me! Allah, the All Merciful, save me!"

The wood before Kennedy was crackling and the heat was growing steadily. A jumping spark fell at Kennedy's foot and his boot began to burn.

Zahr could stand it no longer. "I pardon thee, El Kennedy! On my oath I pardon thee! I admit that thou art a human being!"

"Fire!" ordered Kennedy. "Stop!"

The red tongues reached up to the last of the dark trail and stopped there, finding no more gasoline, unable to eat into the green timbers.

The surface gasoline on Kennedy's boot was burning off. The blaze was getting hot. Kennedy reached down with his tied hands and sawed at the binding cord. It was already halfway through and it came away.

He sprang over the barricade and scuffed his boot in the dust. The flame went out.

But before he could get his breath or realize that this wasn't going to be the finish after all, a thundering avalanche of steel and men and horses bore down upon the pavilion. Kennedy grabbed at a Sudanese and presented his wrists. Without further question, the black hacked the rope with his scimitar.

45

And then Kennedy saw who the horsemen were. El As'ad's troops.

He heard a scream cut through the turmoil and caught a dust-blotted glimpse of Dunya. A trooper snatched up El As'ad.

Chapter Seven

THE cavalry thundered away. It was too swift for immediate comprehension, but Kennedy understood before the others. El As'ad had been afraid of *jinn* magic, but he had made certain of Dunya. With her in his hands, the reputation of Zahr's house would be at stake and Zahr would have to come to terms. Otherwise his daughter would be a slave instead of a married princess.

Kennedy ran toward his ship. The Tuaregs sprang back from his path, staring after him, too dazed to understand what had taken place or what was about to happen. Somewhere behind him Kennedy heard Zahr's roar, heard the hammering of hoofs as pursuit started out. They would follow, even though they knew they would not hope to catch El As'ad.

The ship seemed to be all right until Kennedy glanced under the nose while pulling the prop through. A puddle of gasoline was there. Dunya had been unable to shut off the petcock.

Acting quickly, he shifted to the five gallons in the reserve tank and started the motor. Zahr dashed up, mounted on a plunging white horse.

"Bring her back!" cried Zahr. "Bring her back in your bird and you shall have whatever you wish. He will make a slave of her!"

The engine trebled its roar and the wheels began to move. The Tuaregs had seen it in action once and they scattered from its path. Kennedy thundered straight at the far line of trees. The wind was right, the wings were pulling her off, the wheels jumped from the ground.

He went up in a climbing turn, pulling on his helmet and goggles and flying with his knees. That done, he studied the country under him.

Two long columns of dust, far apart, were in a floored ravine which led deeper into the range. Through their drifting fog, Kennedy caught sight of men and horses and the flash of sun on steel.

The biplane banked steeply and he sped after the cavalry. He did not quite know how he would get Dunya back. Certainly he could kill some of those people from the air, but that would place Dunya under fire. And more than anything else, Kennedy wanted to see El As'ad put away. El As'ad and Es Samad suddenly became everything which had hounded Kennedy for years.

He flew above them, not a hundred feet over their heads. Eyes were raised, afraid, but El As'ad's men rode on. Kennedy banked and came back, circling, wondering how long he could keep this up on five gallons of gas. He had cut his throttle to the last notch possible and the ship was staggering with insufficient flying speed.

A group of horsemen detached themselves at a bend in the ravine. They dismounted, unslinging guns, to jump behind rocks. This was an ambush for Zahr's men.

The biplane headed down, wires shrieking. Kennedy cocked

the guns and let drive. The doll-like men in white started to run, glancing up at the source of the racketing sound. One of them had courage enough to stop and fire his flintlock. The line of bullets went over him and through him and traveled on.

Running like startled sheep down the ravine, El As'ad's men came suddenly into view of Zahr's *mamelukes*.

Kennedy knew that that was the end of the ambush and he turned about, speeding in pursuit of the main body of troops. When he sighted them again they had left the gorge and were entering upon an open plain.

In the distance the sun struck fire from a city which sprawled down a hillside. This would be Hamra.

Kennedy groaned. He could do nothing without endangering Dunya, and his hour's supply of gasoline was rapidly exhausting itself. He doubted, even now, that he had enough for the return to Zahr's city.

His eye picked up a flash on Hamra's outskirts. Another cloud of dust, another troop of cavalry. Evidently Es Samad had expected this coup and had his men ready to cover his son's retreat. The riders came on at a fast run, pennons fluttering.

Kennedy knew that he could and would do something about this. He still had some gas and a few rounds of ammunition at his disposal. Engine snarling, he dived at the massed ranks which were racing toward him.

Mamelukes reined in, staring. The machine guns rolled like kettle drums. Blue tracers ripped through the glinting prop arc. The first and second ranks went down like lines of dominos. Dust closed in over the heads of the remaining troops.

Kennedy did a wingover and came back, guns hammering once more. He saw that the remnants were pounding back toward Hamra, trailed by a hunched figure on a white horse. That would be Es Samad himself!

El As'ad and his men were coming up, cautiously. Kennedy held his fire. The reserve was almost gone and he was almost out of ammunition, but he could still put on a show.

But evidently the troopers were more afraid of El As'ad's penalties than they were of the plane. The columns dashed forward toward the town.

Zahr's troops were galloping out of the pass mouth far behind. Kennedy knew that the city gates would be closed against them before they could ever reach it.

The city gates!

Without wasting a second, Kennedy dived toward the distant towers. Leaning his head into the slipstream, he saw that there was only one gate opening up into the plain. That suited his purpose—if he could only block the gate until Zahr arrived!

CHAPTER EIGHT

K ENNEDY pulled his throttle and dived. Wires shrilled, fabric fluttered as he slipped. Hamra heeled over, came right again and Kennedy pancaked in, lancing towards the gates.

The stone walls loomed; alarmingly the solid gas-starved engine sputtered. Tuaregs lined the battlements. White flame belched from long gun muzzles. A wire parted with a twang.

In a swirl of khaki-colored dust, the ship ground looped within thirty feet of the gate. Kennedy stood up in his pit, waving his arms. The sun flashed from his goggles. The Tuaregs stared with disbelief. Whirling about they plunged away into the heart of the city.

With a tight smile, Kennedy dropped to the ground, picked up the tail and hauled it back toward the opening in the walls. Behind him, Es Samad's *mamelukes* thundered across the plain.

Kennedy dropped the tail between the stone towers. He climbed back into the cockpit and studied the ground before him.

Es Samad was rolling up under a billowing fog of dust. With upraised swords and shining shields, the troopers were applying quirt and spur toward their city. They did not seem to fear the stubby wings which lay between them and their goal. Evidently they were not afraid of it on the ground.

51

Wires shrilled, fabric fluttered as he slipped.
Hamra heeled over, came right again and Kennedy
pancaked in, lancing towards the gates.

Or perhaps the bullying shouts of Es Samad were more greatly to be feared.

Standing in his pit, hands on the top wing, squinting through the shimmering arc of the idling prop, Kennedy saw that El As'ad was closing the distance with his several hundred horsemen. When El As'ad joined forces with his father, their very numbers would encourage them.

Almost a mile away, Zahr's *mamelukes* were coming up, no more than a swirl of dust over sparkling pinpoints of light. Kennedy knew that he would have to wait until Zahr was nearer, otherwise he would have nothing to back him up. And when Zahr did come within striking distance, Kennedy was determined to charge Es Samad with his ship, guns going.

But Es Samad had also seen Zahr's forces and he was determined to occupy his walls to repel the threatened attack. Only one man and a flimsy thing which looked like a bird stood between Hamra's ruler and his objective.

Kennedy knew that once Es Samad succeeded in getting inside the town, nothing short of heavy artillery would dislodge him. And Dunya would stare at blank walls the rest of her life.

The gas gauge was down to the left side of zero. Which meant that less than three minutes of flying time remained. Hardly enough to take off.

And Zahr was still far away.

And Es Samad's *mamelukes* showed no signs of slackening their pace.

Kennedy tugged nervously at his dangling helmet strap. Abruptly a long gash appeared in the fabric of the top wing. Kennedy whirled and stared at the gates. A squad of men were coming across the open toward him. One dropped to his knee and fired. The solid *thwack* of lead through wood sounded at Kennedy's feet.

Seeing no immediate menace in Kennedy, the squad started to run toward him. Behind them came the others, veils whipping, djellabas cracking.

His face tense, Kennedy studied the gate. It was thirty feet wide. Beyond it lay a strip of white pavement.

Turning he saw that Es Samad had stopped. El As'ad's troops drew up on rearing horses. A babble of voices reached Kennedy. El As'ad was screaming that the bird was harmless on the ground, that they should attack instantly before Zahr came.

Es Samad's white horse ran to one side, followed by a compact group of cavalry. El As'ad pointed urgently to the plane and the gates, and then back at Zahr's charging *mamelukes*.

Kennedy clenched his teeth. If only he knew that he wouldn't hit Dunya. The Tuaregs spread out in a long line. A horn bellowed. Hoofs began to pound. Shields and swords and glittering accouterments clashed with the sunlight.

A bullet hacked through a strut. Kennedy glanced back of him to see a score of men on foot almost upon his plane.

And then he caught sight of a fluttering white dress. Es Samad and El As'ad had drawn far to one side, and Dunya was with them!

Kennedy slumped in the pit. He jammed the throttle into the dash. The engines roared. The wheels began to spin across the ground.

Rank on rank of charging cavalry, a nerve-shattering medley of plunging horses and cracking pennons. The prop bored stridently toward the line.

The machine guns chattered, spewing white flame. Empty brass shells leaped into the slipstream. Kennedy pulled back his stick and worked his rudders.

Riders threw up their arms and pitched into the oblivion of dust. Horses stumbled and skidded to a shuddering stop to be immediately beaten under by pounding hoofs.

Kennedy was flying at ten feet. He banked ninety degrees and hammered the line on its flank. Terror-stricken eyes raised up. Mounts bolted. Tuaregs laid on their whips in a scurrying attempt to get away from the snarling bird above them.

The gas needle went to the center of zero. The engine faltered, picked up and faltered again.

Kennedy looked toward the spot he had last seen El As'ad. And El As'ad was gone!

The small group was streaking toward the gates, had almost reached them. Kennedy felt the plane sag under him. The engine was sputtering and coughing, dragging its last breaths.

Kennedy banked with his wing tip caressing the turf. With a heart-stopping lurch, the ship slipped sideways. He slammed on the starboard aileron, righted it. And then he saw that in the excitement he had misjudged the distance.

With flying speed gone, unable to turn, he watched the walls rush at him over his dead prop. A bank would be suicide. He could not stop before he reached the battlements.

Glancing anxiously behind him he saw that Zahr would

never make it in time. El As'ad and Dunya would be inside the city, behind closed gates, within the next ten seconds.

The sigh of wires was shrill in the silence about him. Kennedy drew a long breath and waited for the shattering crash which would come before he could draw his next.

And then he saw the gates. Thirty feet across and his wing spread was thirty-five. Better to reduce his speed by taking off his wings. Better to make his plane a flaming block to prevent the closing of the portals.

The watchtowers whipped up at him. A current of air unexpectedly bolstered his wings. Not daring to breathe, Kennedy slanted over. He could see the faces of men above him on the walls; he could see the greedy stone rushing up to smash him.

He swallowed hard and took a lungful of air. The pavement was under his wheels. Automatically he leveled out, unable to believe that he had actually verticaled between those two watchtowers.

Ahead of him Es Samad and the handful of soldiers were racing away, looking back with horror-widened eyes.

Kennedy's wheels crunched against the pavement. Something like a smile flitted across his smoke-grimed face. He ruddered slightly, following El As'ad with the taxiing ship.

El As'ad's uneven teeth were chattering with terror. Suddenly his nerve broke. He reined in, throwing up his hands as though in prayer. His shrill voice cracked.

"Save me! Spare me!" wailed El As'ad.

Kennedy ground looped and stopped. He stood up in the

pit, facing El As'ad. Es Samad and the others had also come to a stop.

The *mamelukes* were throwing down their swords and holding up their hands to show that they were no longer armed.

Something white detached itself from a trooper's saddle and ran towards the ship.

Dunya!

She came in close to the cockpit and stood looking up at Kennedy, her gray eyes adoring him and thanking him.

Kennedy's voice was loud and assured. "Es Samad! I call upon you to surrender yourself and your kingdom to me, Abd El Kennedy."

El As'ad's twisted body seemed to shrink. His white horse moved nervously. Meekly, Es Samad replied, "I surrender."

From the gate came the sound of advancing hoofs.

Zahr, flanked by his legions of *mamelukes*, glared at Es Samad. "Dismount, unworthy one. Allah's justice has reached you at last. From this time henceforth you shall rule only the mice in your dungeon."

Zahr turned upon the shivering El As'ad. "And you, misbegotten ape, shall keep your father company. Had it not been for your knavery I would have allowed you to rule.

"But now, as was once the case, the state of Hamra again becomes a province of my kingdom."

Zahr raised his hand to his *mamelukes*. "Take these two prisoners and escort them to my city. Disarm Es Samad's *mamelukes* to prevent them from rising against us."

Kennedy stepped down from the pit and took Dunya's arm.

Zahr dismounted and approached them.

Kennedy was smiling. "You told me anything I wanted was mine, Zahr. Do you admit now that I am a human being?"

"How can I, after this performance, El Kennedy? But you are either a valorous, clever young knight or a *jinnī*. I prefer to think of you as the former. What is it you want?"

"Dunya."

Zahr nodded. "Upon my oath before Allah, I know of nothing better than to have you as my crown prince."

"And two horses for Dunya and myself," added Kennedy.

"But what is the matter with your bird?"

Kennedy turned and looked at his ship. "It will have to be carried back to your city. Perhaps some day, if I send by caravan for a certain substance, it will fly again. But now it will not."

"Then," cried Zahr, laughing, "it is man-made after all! Then that proves that you are not a *jinnī*! If you were— Come, there is a wedding ceremony all arranged and it will be simple to complete it."

Dunya's smiling eyes were looking up at him and Kennedy smiled back, taking her arm and gently squeezing it.

When he mounted his horse, Kennedy thought to himself that quiet would prevail in these two realms while he was there. They were afraid of his bird and of himself.

Trotting across the plain toward Zahr's city with Lady Dunya at his side, Kennedy knew that he had, at last, found peace.

BUCKLEY PLAYS A HUNCH

BUCKLEY PLAYS A HUNCH

CALL it foresight, perspicuity, prevision or just a plain hunch. Whatever its title, Jim Buckley had it. He could feel it creep over him like snake coils. All was not well on that island.

The instant the beacon fire had leaped up on the headland, in spite of the months he had searched for just that signal, an intangible inner voice had told him it was wrong.

But Jim Buckley managed a thin smile and tried to make himself feel some of the joy he had told himself he would experience. Just a column of thick smoke pivoting over yellow flame. Just a blot against the fantastic shapes of low-hung clouds. The signal he had been watching for night and day—in fact, constantly since he had taken the job "Old Man" Derring had offered him in San Francisco.

"Find them," Derring had growled. "They're still alive. They must be. Comb the Solomons, the Societies, the Fijis and every damned island that shoves its nose out of the Pacific."

Those had been his orders and now, sailing straight into the northern Marianas group, Jim Buckley was at the end of his trail. After months of wandering, after months of being buffeted about by storm and calm in a seventy-foot boat, he knew his quest was over.

There in the afternoon quiet, lighted solely for his benefit, was the beacon. He had found the lost expedition. He had found Sutter, Joyce, Hadron and Gillespie. And still—his hair crawled and he wanted to turn and run for it.

The Polynesian at the wheel felt none of it. He grinned good-naturedly and nodded. He too, had grown tired of this searching. Just two men in a small boat, looking forever on the other side of receding horizons. The Polynesian grinned, and Jim Buckley tried to grin back.

The yawl bubbled forward, leaving a white path on the incredible blue sea. The booms creaked and the canvas cracked when the bowsprit headed for a trough. The forgotten island with its smoke beacon gradually spread out and engulfed the horizon.

Buckley chose a cove and headed in, finding a reef passage where none appeared to be, trusting to the sixth or seventh sense of the sailor to put the yawl into the quiet water near the beach.

All sails in, the Polynesian dropped the dinghy into the water and stood by, ready to cast off.

But Buckley shook his head. "Stay with the ship, laddie. We may have need of getting under way smartly."

The Polynesian nodded briefly and blinked when he saw Buckley drape a rifle over his shoulder and buckle on a pistol belt—for this was the first time he had ever seen his white man arm himself.

And then Buckley dropped into the tender and rowed away toward the white sand and curving palms, toward a spot where three men had suddenly appeared among the trees.

Before he landed, Buckley turned and looked at them; turned and saw them wave to him. Three men in rags, looking gaunt and yellow and sick. Three men with beards on their faces and black hair matted on their chests. Just three starved white men, but Buckley found himself reluctant to land. It wasn't usual, that feeling, and Buckley fought it down. He swore at himself, pulled hard on the oars and heard sand grate under the dinghy keel.

They were around him immediately, their eyes filled with disbelief. And Buckley was suddenly ashamed of his own clean ducks, his shaved face, his pipe-clayed helmet and most of all, his guns.

"Derring sent me," Buckley said.

Three pairs of eyes swept over him and held him down.

"Derring?" said one, and then began to laugh. "Derring sent you? To find us?"

The others were serious and watchful, and Buckley looked at them, frowning. He knew then that these men must be a little mad. Slightly crazed by starvation, fever, isolation.

"Yes," he said. "Of course Derring sent me. Get your baggage if you have any. We'll sail on this tide."

"Baggage?" said another, staring, arms hanging listlessly.

And then the first to speak stopped laughing. "See here," he said. "I'm forgetting my manners. I'm Hadron. Professor G. C. Hadron. This tall one is Mr. D. M. Joyce. And this is Sutter, our engineer."

"I'm Buckley. Pleased to meet all of you." He felt uneasy, unwanted. Here were no thanks for rescue. No evidence of extreme joy at being picked up.

"But we can't go tonight," said Joyce hoarsely. "Can't possibly make it. Business, you know." It was as if he had just concluded an argument of great length.

"Specimens, I suppose," said Buckley. "And you've been here so long one more night won't make any difference. Let's go up to your camp and I'll lend you a hand."

The three turned instantly and shuffled away in single file. They didn't look back to see if Buckley followed. If they had, they would have seen him standing, his eyes squinted, his lips pursed. With a puzzled shake of his head, he trailed them.

The camp was on a high point of land, but hidden. Several crude shacks stood about a littered clearing. Weathered boxes were stacked in ragged piles. A corroded microscope lay beside a pile of ashes, battered from its long service of lighting fires.

"So Derring sent you," said Hadron and laughed. "He didn't forget us, after all." And then, so quickly that Buckley almost dodged, he ran into a hut and came out with his hands full of papers. "Credentials," he chuckled. "Lots of credentials. Look at them."

His face a blank, sitting half crouched ready for a spring, Buckley took the sheafs and inspected them. They were letters from Derring to Hadron, Joyce, Gillespie and Sutter. They promised ample funds for the outfitting of a schooner and bade godspeed to the expedition in its search for Pacific archaeological artifacts.

"Now," said Hadron, triumphantly, "where are your credentials?"

Buckley wanted to swear, but the certain cold knowledge

that these men were mad stopped him. Three pairs of eyes were heavy on him. "On the *Crusader*," he said. "I'll show them to you in the morning. Hadn't you better start getting your stuff together?"

"He calls it 'stuff,'" said Joyce despairingly.

But Buckley paid no heed. "Where is Gillespie?"

"Dead," Hadron snapped. "Stone dead from fever. If you hadn't been so long coming for us—" He stopped suddenly, laughed in loud, whooping gusts of mirth.

"You stay here tonight," Joyce said. "Stay here in that shack over there. Tomorrow we'll catch the tide and go. We have much packing to do. Much packing. Work." He nodded, over-brightly.

And Buckley, five foot six, immaculate, sat very still and watched them go about the preparation of an evening meal. Only once after that did he venture a question to Hadron.

"What happened to Parker, the second mate?" he asked.

"Dead," snapped Hadron, pausing in his restless movements around the fire. "Buried him at sea. The rest died when we ran the *Dolphin* on the reef. She didn't wait long to sink. Damned if she did."

Jim Buckley nodded, his eyes a little hard.

Drowsing on a pile of dry grass in the dubious shelter of a shack, Buckley gave way to a feeling of sorrow. Somehow he felt that he had failed. Of course, he could not help the condition of the scientists, but nevertheless he held himself responsible. If he had only looked here first instead of last he

65

might have saved their sanity. Still, there had been no way of telling where they were. Their route had been indefinite, their communications far between.

On leaving Samoa they had headed west, and that had been the last report on the *Dolphin* for nearly two years.

Derring had also felt responsible. It had been his thousands which had made this expedition possible, and had sent Jim Buckley out on the long quest. Derring had placed all his hopes in Buckley, and now, Buckley told himself, he had let Derring down.

And then his musings were cut off for an instant by a sound of whispering on the still, black air of night. The three were in another shack almost a hundred feet away and yet their words came clearly through the darkness.

"What will we do with the treasure?" whispered the hoarse voice which belonged to Sutter.

The chuckle was Hadron's. "Take it. We can do it now."

"Fine," rasped Joyce.

That was all, but it deepened the sensation of sadness which had grown upon Buckley. Madness, all of it. They thought they had treasure. They were babbling excitedly about riches which did not exist. They were mad.

And Buckley slept, lightly as always. He was curled in a compact mass under the tarpaulin, one hand resting on his automatic, the other on the bolt of his rifle. He was used to sleeping that way, and in spite of the spring tension of his wiry body, he rested well.

The night deepened. Far away the surf was mumbling its

undying chant against the reef. An occasional puff of hot wind clattered the palm fronds about the clearing. And then something else which was not wind rustled stealthily.

Instantly, Buckley was awake and ready. He tightened the pistol belt about his slim waist and slid silently out from beneath the canvas. Rolling, he removed himself from the vicinity of the crude bed. He didn't ask himself why he did so or what the new noise might be. He merely obeyed an impulse which told him to move.

For many dragging seconds he lay still, listening and waiting. Wind rustled the bony fronds; the surf droned. Buckley stared up into blackness, waiting. A minute went past. Then another. A third, a fourth.

Tightly, Buckley rolled back to his bed, hand outstretched to encounter something which was so cold and hard that its touch produced a shock as physical as pain.

He examined it with his fingers. Hilt upright, a knife was buried in his bed. Seven inches of steel buried where he had lain a few minutes before. Someone had attempted to murder him and had missed by a margin so narrow that sweat started out on Buckley's brow.

His first impulse was to run out and mop up the entire outfit, but he fought it down. Cautiously he bent himself into a sitting posture and waited. Certainly, if they thought he was dead, they would return for his guns.

Managing to convince himself of that, he sat very still and ready. But nothing happened. There was only pounding surf and rustling wind and blackness.

And then Buckley knew that something else had occurred. Just what, he was not aware. He knew that the camp was deserted. Slowly he stood up and stepped out through the door, fumbling for the unaccustomed objects in his path. He made his way to the shack where the three had slept, but no sound of breathing came to him.

The cold conviction of his fate was upon him. The shack was empty. Buckley spun about and loosened the gun in its holster. With distance-eating strides he went down the twisting trail to the beach.

Creepers caught at his ankles. Thorns tore at his clothes. He lost the trail again and again, but each time located it. Gradually, acting as a compass, the pound of the surf grew louder. And then loose sand was under his feet and ripples were phosphorescent in front of him.

But the ripples were empty. Buckley searched quickly for the tender, but it was gone. He stopped and looked out toward the reef, submerged by the tide.

No glimmer of white out there. No sound of oars or sails. Nothing but black night. Buckley knew then how it felt to be marooned; how it felt to have thousands of miles between himself and home with no way to traverse them; how it felt to look ahead into empty days of idleness and hope—vague hope. He knew he would prepare a beacon he could touch off when a ship came near. That he would watch many a hull sink blindly over the horizon before he was taken off.

His ship was gone. The three madmen had taken it after trying to murder him. And Buckley stood with a blank face and stared into the dark, his jaw set, his wiry body tense with anger.

This was his pay. This was what he got in return for months of grinding search. He'd found them and they, with some hallucination of treasure, had gone and left him, thinking him dead. Madmen.

He threw back his head and looked at the Southern Cross as if it might answer his unspoken question. And strangely enough, it did. Buckley knew then that he was not alone on this island. Someone else was here with him. Not close at hand. Perhaps miles away. But he was not alone. And of natives there were none. Only the white castaways. But Buckley took a deep breath and played his hand as it lay upon fate's gaming table.

He turned to the north and began to walk. Not too fast, for that would tire him, but with long, swinging strides which looked all out of proportion to his size.

He had never owned himself licked; he wouldn't now. No use to give in and sit down and weep crocodile tears. Nothing to do but plow on and grab any straw which might be cast up on this beach.

The east first turned purple. The clouds became less vague and began to stand out and color in fantastic animal shapes. Slowly the water took up the reflection and the wind died utterly, leaving the world in the dim silence of dawn. With the suddenness of a bombardment, the world turned completely light and the day had come.

Buckley stopped and cast his eyes restlessly over the horizon for a sail he knew he would not find. The *Crusader* would be gone by now. There had been enough of a breeze to push her light heels along. The Polynesian would probably float up on the sands in a day or so. Buckley promised himself that he would search for the body and give it a decent burial.

But the sound of a shot put an end to his musing. It was the hollow, coughing sound that a rifle makes in the open.

Deliberately, Buckley strode up the grade of the beach and stepped into the underbrush out of sight. Another shot sent an undulating cloud of gray gulls up from the water.

Satisfied that the shots had not been meant for him, Buckley jacked a cartridge into his rifle and snapped on the safety catch. Whoever had done the shooting had been very near. Hope flicked hungrily in the back of his brain.

There were other snapping cracks ahead of him, growing nearer as he walked. And then he stopped when he heard the rumbling of a rock rolling down a hill. The thunder stopped, and another rifle spat on Buckley's left.

Lips tight, rifle ready for whatever might come, he slipped from tree to tree, his small wiry body offering no target in spite of his white clothes. Ahead, a space of light in the tangle indicated the presence of a clearing. Slower, silent, and ready, he slipped to the edge and stood motionless.

Joyce was there. Joyce with his matted beard, his sunken cheeks, his fever-bright eyes. In his hands was a rifle, and while Buckley watched, the gun slanted up and hurled a singing slug up the barren hillside.

The jungle ended here at the edge of this mountain. A ledge

of limestone acted as a barricade against some unseen force. And then a boulder, starting slow, rumbled down, crushing the grass in its path to come to rest against a papaya tree. The large, green fruit clumped out of the shaken branches and rolled listlessly on their sides.

Whatever Joyce might be fighting, Buckley didn't know. He merely knew that here was one of those who had attempted to murder him. Why the man wasn't with the schooner, or where the schooner might be, did not concern Buckley at that moment. Probably there had been a falling out among the three and this was the result. Probably Joyce was as much a castaway now as ever. The rifle had come from the cabin of the *Crusader*.

Buckley spoke, his voice low and even: "Turn around, Joyce."

Joyce turned, his ragged mouth slacked, his eyes incredibly wide.

"Drop your gun," said Buckley, without any trace of emotion. Inside, he felt regretful at having to manhandle the fellow. But he had been hired to bring them back, and he was trying to do his job.

The rifle sagged and almost slipped out of the castaway's fingers. And then, like a striking snake, it came up to hip level and spat a venomous tongue of flame.

Buckley didn't shoot. He weaved to one side, dropped his own rifle and launched himself like a white javelin. His outstretched hands encircled the other's waist, hurling him back.

Joyce grunted and shifted his feet to catch himself. He

71

was a full head taller than Buckley. Once more Joyce tried to lift the rifle. But Buckley was the faster of the two. He stepped back and his fist described a swift, blurred arc. It mushroomed out the other's beard. Buckley struck again and stepped back, ready, waiting.

But the castaway's wrists bent; his head sagged forward, and his long body doubled like a jackknife. Joyce was sprawled out, moaning.

Creepers were near at hand, and Buckley bent regretfully to his task of tying Joyce. It saddened him, this having to strike down men without their reason. They did not know what they did. They were victims of isolation and fever and starvation. Perhaps some day they would recover their reason if the schooner was still there to take them home.

Another rifle was firing methodically several hundred feet away. Other stones were rumbling down the hillside. But Buckley completed a careful job of tying his captive before he furthered his campaign.

He wrinkled his brow in wonder at the situation, but he knew all that would be solved as soon as he collected the combatants. Leaving Joyce to his moans, Buckley worked his way toward the sound of the other rifle.

On the edge of the jungle, facing the source of the rocks, Hadron was chuckling to himself and firing with a cold, deliberate eye. His gun was only a .22, but he held it in sling and squeezed the trigger with great care. This weapon had also come from the cabin of the *Crusader*.

Buckley changed his tactics. He knew that these men had no fear in their madness. He knew that he had no power over them but his fists. He could not shoot them, for how would he ever explain it if he did?

He stepped up within a foot of Hadron before his presence was detected. Hadron whirled with a questioning roar and his arms were suddenly crushed tight to his sides. Buckley grunted with the exertion and slued the man around, throwing him backward, where he tripped and fell.

But Hadron was up in an instant. No recognition on his face. Nothing but the desire to kill. Buckley struck at the massive face and struck again. Hadron weaved slightly and came on. And then Buckley pulled his fist all the way from the ground and snapped Hadron's head back until the eyes bulged.

Kneeling beside the prostrate body, Buckley started to secure the man with dry creepers. Stones were bouncing off the ledge and crashing into the jungle behind, but he knew that he was not in their range, although he could not refrain from the practice of looking up each time one hit.

All was not well about him, and Buckley knew it with a certainty which lent haste to his flying hands. As yet he did not know where his schooner was, or just what these two castaways had thought they might gain by staying on the island. Perhaps Sutter was up there on the hill, rolling the rocks down in a vain, idiotic attempt to keep all the "treasure" for himself.

However, Sutter was there within five feet of Buckley before he made his presence known. The sound of a footfall made Buckley dart to one side. Quickly, his hand on his automatic, he glanced up.

The sound of a footfall made Buckley dart to one side.
Quickly, his hand on his automatic, he glanced up.

Sutter made a motion with his gun for Buckley to stand upright. The weapon was a small target pistol, also from the *Crusader*.

"You shouldn't do that," said Sutter, his tones hoarse and dull, his eyes reproachful.

From the mere look of the man, Buckley wanted to laugh himself. But, instead, he closed his mouth trap like and waited.

"We've got to get the treasure," said Sutter. "You've got no right—"

Buckley was moving slowly around in a circle, keeping his distance from Sutter, doing nothing which would cause the man to shoot. Sutter pivoted with him, still talking, until his back was against the source of the occasional stones.

And then Buckley began to back slowly away. Sutter moved with him. A rock bounded down close beside the castaway, but he glanced disinterestedly at it. Another struck close by, coming to a rest beside Buckley's feet.

"Where is the schooner?" Buckley asked.

"Oh, that's gone," Sutter replied. "We sank it. It was too—" The sentence was never finished. A bounding rock struck Sutter between the shoulder blades and catapulted him straight into Buckley's waiting arms.

Gently, Buckley laid the man down and tied him up. That done, he stood looking at the hillside and at the stones which still rolled in abundance. His brows were furrowed.

Hadron had come to and was laughing softly to himself at some joke that he himself could not explain. He caught sight of his captor and laughed more loudly.

"You think you can get away with the treasure," chuckled

Hadron. "They won't ever let you. They'll hammer you down with those rocks. They want it all for themselves."

"They?" asked Buckley.

"Sure. Go on up and find out. They'll get you quick enough." And then Hadron went off into another spasm of laughter.

Buckley straightened himself, adjusted his helmet and pulled a handkerchief out of his pocket. If those were natives or some more of the insane crowd, they would make short work of him. But there might be something else which he should know. Certainly he had little enough to take back to Derring. A hunch set his face toward the hillside and he began to move.

Twice he waved the white handkerchief, but if any one had ever hidden behind those rock barricades, they did not answer. Buckley shrugged and tucked the linen into his ducks, knowing in a bleak way that he made a fine target for an avalanche. He changed his course and ascended diagonally, inspecting his goal.

Caves were up there. A long line of them carved out by wind and sea which had removed the softer content of the rock. In front of these, in long lines, were man-made barricades silently sheltering eyes which Buckley could feel but could not see.

Buckley went on. The sun was hot on his back and the sweat was dripping out of his helmet into his eyes. At any moment he expected rocks to come bounding down at him. Saw-grass cut at his white trousers. Thorns ripped his shirt sleeves. And still no sign of life within the caves.

He changed his course again, heading for the end of the

barricade. He knew he was being watched and his expression was a blank save for the darting of his dark blue eyes. His hand swung casually close to the pistol at his side.

And then he had arrived at a level with the caves. An engulfing wave of surprise brought him to a rigid stop. Lying in a neat row were the disconnected and bleached frames of a dozen men. The skulls stared sightless at the dazzling sky, jaws agape. Even in that brief instant of amazed scrutiny, Buckley saw that the beings were of tremendous size. Giants they were, fully eight feet long. And on the bleached forehead of each was a number.

A bluff, rumbling voice whipped at him out of nowhere. "Who the hell are you?"

For an instant Buckley keyed himself to fight it out, but before he could throw himself down, a man appeared from behind a rock. A clean-shaven face, wind-burned and heavy. Tattered clothes flapping whitely in the faint breeze.

"I'm Jim Buckley."

The other's brows came down heavily. "What are you doing here?"

Buckley's head came back and his eyes seemed to travel straight through the other's body. "I was sent out by Derring to find—"

"The hell you say!" The man whirled about and shouted behind him at others, who immediately jumped into sight. There were four of them in all. Elderly, intelligent and clean.

"I'm Hadron," rumbled the first to speak, extending his hand. "These others are Sutter, Gillespie and Joyce. I knew Derring would send out to find us."

The three crowded around, silent, their eyes filled with disbelief. Joyce reached out and touched Buckley on the shoulder, suddenly smiling.

"I knew Derring wouldn't let us down," said Joyce. "I knew he wouldn't. Is that your schooner down there in the cove?"

Buckley looked and then breathed a deep sigh of relief. The *Crusader* was riding easily at anchor just inside the reef and upon her afterdeck a brown body moved. Evidently his Polynesian had wormed himself out of his bonds, or perhaps had not been tied at all.

Sutter and Gillespie had sunk weakly down upon large stones, staring at each other. They were free now. Released from this island which had held them prisoner for so many torturous months. They were free, but they could not readily realize it.

Joyce went over to the skeletons and began to place them gently in palm baskets. Hadron stood and looked at Buckley.

"Artifacts?" asked Buckley, pointing at the bones.

And this jarred Hadron back into his bluff, hearty self. "Hell, yes! We've got enough material to keep us busy for years. Eight-foot men, Buckley. Think of it. We've got the lost history of the Pacific in our hip pockets. That should make Derring whoop for joy, shouldn't it? Oh, we haven't been idle. Far from it. Since the day those devils ran the schooner on a reef—"

"Oh, so they were aboard your ship?"

"Sure they were. We picked them off an island south of here. Crazy as coots. Where are they now?"

Buckley pointed at the foot of the hill. "I tied them up."

"You did!" And Hadron looked at Buckley's five feet six. "Lucky you didn't run into their camp. They'd have murdered you."

"I spent the night there, and they tried hard enough to kill me."

"You—Listen, Joyce. He spent the night with those damned loons!"

"Yes," said Buckley. "They told me they were you and I almost believed them. I sailed into the other side of the island and they met me on the beach."

"So that's why we didn't see you. We're miles away from their camp."

"They thought you had some treasure up here. That's why they were so persistent about attacking you."

Hadron's brows shot up. "Treasure?" And then he smiled. "I suppose they overheard us talking about valuable material on the boat. All treasure isn't gold, you know. Those skeletons are worth thousands. And the other material is without price."

Buckley nodded and then turned to look once more at his schooner. "I'd better be going down. There's a tide this afternoon and if you get all your material aboard, we can make it. You know, I almost sailed without you yesterday."

Hadron seemed to shiver. "Why didn't you?"

"Hunch," replied Buckley. "When I beached my tender I knew those fellows were crazy, and I almost cracked down on them with a gun. Almost loaded them aboard by force. But something was wrong. I knew there was. Especially when they told me that Parker had died."

"There wasn't any Parker with us!"

"Of course there wasn't. That's why I stuck around. I did think they were you all right, but something told me not to take them away. I didn't and here I am."

"Hunch," said Hadron, and laid a hand on Buckley's shoulder. "I had one and it told me not to take those fellows off that island. But I didn't play it, and look what happened."

"Sure," replied Buckley. "I guess I'd better be getting back to the schooner." He turned and trudged down the hillside toward the growing drone of the waves.

It was as though a ton weight had been lifted from his shoulders. He threw them back. The sky was bluer and the island seemed bright with color. Something he hadn't noticed before. He hadn't failed after all. He could take the lost expedition back to Derring intact.

For a moment he paused at the jungle's edge and looked down at the three bound castaways who would soon be placed aboard en route to an insane asylum.

The man who had called himself Hadron gazed at the palm fronds high above him and laughed. He was unaware of Buckley. He had forgotten about the treasure as he had forgotten the point of his priceless joke.

Buckley picked him up and threw him over his shoulder with a practiced swing. In spite of the heavy load, Buckley tramped steadily down the trail.

The castaway's laughter blended with the swelling roar of the surf.

MEDALS FOR MAHONEY

MEDALS FOR MAHONEY

"MAHONEY, my boy," said Mahoney, squinting down the hot barrel of the rifle, "if you do say so yourself, you aren't such a bad shot."

The Polynesian up the palm had a gilded body and a shock of red-dyed hair, a perfect silhouette against the flame-blue sky. He was in the act of waving a message to his fellows who were masked by the steamy jungle.

Mahoney set his windage with a calloused thumb, placed his black eye impersonally to the number ten peep and gently contracted his whole hand around the trigger. The steel-shod butt slammed against his bruised shoulder.

The arm waved once more. It jerked up and flopped back. The native was pried away, headfirst, from the gray palm bark. He plummeted out of sight.

"No, Mahoney," said Mahoney, "I've certainly seen worse."

He left the north side of the warehouse loft and went to the partly open door at the south. He peered through that a moment or two and then, satisfied that that point was unassailed, he left it and went to the east window.

"Ah," said Mahoney, raising his brows in reproving surprise.

Two copper-colored men were slinking out of the undergrowth on all fours. Their eyes were resolutely fastened

83

upon the main door of the warehouse. One carried a machete, the other dragged a log which might be used for a battering ram.

Mahoney pulled back the bolt, took a clip out of his leather cartridge belt and sent all five shells rattling into the magazine. Raising himself with extreme caution, he sighted the base of the first native's neck.

The rifle jarred. The native's head flopped. The other sprinted back into cover, leaving his companion to stain the glossy green grass a gaudy red.

Mahoney made a face and went to the west window. He decided that this fight would be all right were it not for this endless tramping back and forth through the loft.

Just why they hadn't heard this shooting at the beach he could not understand. Certainly this silent jungle would carry a shot two miles. Perhaps they weren't so interested in the welfare of their last addition to the company. Anderson, general manager of the Kamling Island branch of the Banda Trading Co., had not been overly cordial.

Which reminded Mahoney that he had not yet had time to read his letter of instruction. But then, time was precious in this one-man war. He wished it would rain. He was getting tired of walking.

He peered at the jungle edge, watching for red hair and snaky brown backs. Something *twanged*. A steel-shod arrow barely missed his chin, embedding itself in the window frame. It sang as it quivered. Mahoney saw a groove running along the point. Poison, eh?

No, Anderson wasn't so very anxious, it seemed. And clerks

had been dying off here in Kamling at a rate which had made even hard-boiled Murray raise his brow. When Murray had sent Mahoney to Kamling, he had said:

"Mahoney, you're bored around here. Go on down to Kamling and see what's happening to Anderson's layout. They're stealing him blind with their attacks."

"Well, Mahoney," said Mahoney, readjusting his sights, "nobody can say you're bored now."

These people weren't enjoying this fight. Too many casualties. And for each casualty, they probably planned some new stunt to play upon this latest clerk when they caught him.

Mahoney stopped in the middle of the creaky, musty floor and mopped at his face with a red bandana. It was so damned hot! He wished it would rain. But then when the southeast monsoon came up, and when the rain really did start, it would bring fever.

Mahoney decided he would rather sweat from heat than shiver with malaria. Funny Anderson didn't come. All these trade goods were worth some kind of a fight.

Stumbling across the loose boards through the gloom, he went to the north window once more. Moans were loud out there. Maybe they were carrying off that youngster he'd shot out of the palm.

Mahoney felt his cartridge belt. The pouches were flabby. Only twenty rounds to go. Well, the belt was lighter anyway and he wasn't sweating so hard under it.

His rumpled black hair was plastered against his forehead. From two glistening ends there dripped a silvery series of drops. Occasionally they stung his eyes, but it was much too hot to swear. His breeches clung stickily to his legs and his boots were twin furnaces.

Three tall men leaped out of the undergrowth, shouting and waving spears. Colored feathers jumped up and down on their heads and gold bracelets jangled on their wrists.

Mahoney asked for nothing more. The rifle leaped and spat white flame into the scorching sunlight. One went down, screaming. The other two vanished like smoke.

"Now, pray tell," said Mahoney, "what was the reason for that foray?"

He knew instantly. Jumping up, he ran over to the east window. En route, he stumbled against a pile of boxes, sent their contents jangling across the splintery boards. He swore and jumped up to the casement.

Five men were hammering on the door below. At the edge of the undergrowth a sea of faces peered forth. With a twang, bowstrings cut loose. Mahoney ducked the whistling barrage and tried to get a shot straight down. A spear snapped its copper tip against the tin side of the warehouse.

More men ran out. Smoke and sparks came from their hands. Torches! They plunged sharp points into the heavy doors and sprinted back to the jungle.

Mahoney fired twice and then, except for the three men sprawled limply on the grass, the jungle was deserted. The torches burned quickly down toward the wood. In a moment the wood began to char.

If the door were burned, entrance would be a simple thing. Mahoney looked about the loft. Two buckets of water—all the water in the place—stood under the sloping eaves. He grabbed one and spilled the contents down the wall.

The torches went out.

What the devil was the matter with Anderson? Was he always so careless of his clerks? That young boy Harris, whose place Mahoney was taking, hadn't lasted very long. The fever, Anderson had said, and it hadn't been in the southeast monsoons either.

Mahoney went back to the north window. Something grated under his feet—something which sparkled dully. He scooped up a handful and held them to the light. Lead and brass medals of some long-forgotten fair. Bicycle racing, potato racing—

Standard trade goods, used by the Banda Trading Co. to flimflam the natives out of trepang, gold dust and tortoise shells.

Mahoney tossed the things back out of his road. It would take these fellows a while to summon up nerve for another attack. They were possessed of a stubbornness born of a mixed breed. They were Malays and Papuans and Polynesians all in one and the worst qualities showed up in a fight. It was hard to believe that these same fellows had been peacefully bargaining with him not twenty-four hours before.

Mahoney was puzzled as to their sudden change of spirit. Had the sight of all these trade goods gotten the best of their good sense? Certainly they'd seen this rifle hanging on the wall, and they'd seen his .45 against his hip. They knew what those things meant all right.

But why the devil didn't Anderson pull his freight up here

with a handful of soldiers? Did Anderson think that those soldiers had been hired out of unemployment propaganda? Or maybe Anderson was too busy taking a snooze down on the dock. If he didn't come pretty soon, there'd be a very mangled clerk here who'd been named Mahoney.

A buzz of voices came out of the green foliage, indistinct but indignant. A council of war, most likely, figuring out what they'd do with him when they got him and how they were going to get him.

The voices became louder, more excited. Maybe this was an attempt to cover up another attack.

A patch of white was moving along the trail from the inland side. "I'll nip this," said Mahoney, "while the nipping is good. Mahoney, do your stuff."

The rifle peep focused on the white spot. The trigger came smoothly back. The white spot leaped and Mahoney rubbed his right shoulder. It was getting pretty bruised.

A roar came out of the jungle. "Mahoney! What the hell's the big idea? This is Anderson!"

"Come ahead," shouted Mahoney.

A tall man in dirty whites loped out of the undergrowth, followed by a dozen blacks who carried their rifles at port. Mahoney clattered down the stairs and threw open the double doors.

Anderson lunged into the dim interior. He was thin and sallow and his black stubble emphasized the pallor of his lean face. His eyes were small, surrounded by contour lines netted by squinting through a haze of sunlight half his life. A black pistol stood out from his thigh.

He shook his sun helmet in Mahoney's face. Mahoney saw a bullet hole through the pith crown.

"I just paid thirty dollars for this in Sydney!" shouted Anderson. "And what's the big idea trying to murder me?"

"If I'd known that was you," said Mahoney, "and if I'd wanted to murder you, believe me, I'd have done a better job of it."

"Oh, a wise punk, eh? One of these smart guys Murray picks up in the pink tea joints in Shanghai. Well, you'll soon get that taken out of you."

"You were long enough getting here," replied Mahoney, leaning on his rifle. "What happened to those natives?"

"They—they scattered out as soon as I came along. They're scared of me. And now what was the idea of firing on them? Trying to wreck all the trade I've been years building up?"

"When I went down to the spring to get water this morning, an arrow missed me by two and one-half inches."

"Yeah? Well, I'll bet you didn't stay around long enough to measure it. Look what you've done!" cried Anderson, pointing out at the brown bodies. "They'll carry this war all the way through. They won't be satisfied until they take you and cut you up into little pieces and scatter you into a stew pot."

"I didn't know it was all in fun," said Mahoney.

"Didn't you read my letter of instruction?"

"No, I didn't have time."

"Well, if you didn't read it, hand it over."

Mahoney shoved the dirty, sweat-stained envelope at him. Anderson thrust it into his white coat and then pointed toward the beach two miles away.

"Okay," said Anderson, "if you're so tough, you can hoof it back to the docks. I think you'll catch the next lugger out of here—that is, if you get to the docks."

"What's the idea?" snapped Mahoney. "Aren't you going to let me have a soldier or two? Those devils will jump—"

"Naw, you ain't going to get any soldiers. If you're such a tough fighter, play ball with the boys out in the open."

"Look here, Anderson, I have authority—"

"I don't care if you've got the mumps. Head out there and see if you can get through. If they get you, okay. They'll be satisfied and I won't have to go to all the trouble of making peace with them. Go on, beat it!"

"And if I don't beat it?" Mahoney started to raise the rifle. The black soldiers covered him from four sides. Their sweat-greased faces were quite impassive.

Anderson pointed out at the jungle. "What are you waiting for?"

"For a chance to blow you into little, teeny-weeny bits. If I hadn't taken such a rotten shot, this wouldn't have happened."

The blacks shoved Mahoney into the open. The blank jungle wall seemed to have eyes which glared. Mahoney felt very naked.

"Okay, Mahoney," said Mahoney, "you seen your duty and you done it."

Slipping the rifle sling over his arm and loosening the .45 in its holster, he breasted the tearing undergrowth and wallowed through the tangle of leaves, branches and vines.

Spara momentos—those ugly branches which have their thorns in reverse like fishhooks—dragged him back. There was a path here someplace but Mahoney wasn't very anxious for a path. They'd wait for him along that.

It would be impossible to get through to the beach, but he'd try. Damn that Anderson! The guy was fever-silly. Of course, Mahoney knew he could have pulled the letter from Murray on Anderson, but there was something weird going on here and maybe the letter would have been a speedy passport to Hades.

The hazy twilight was thickened by the rising steam which came from green-scummed pools left from the last rain. Things moved sluggishly out of his path. Occasionally he felt something strike at his ankle but his boots were thick and snakeproof.

The silence weighed down on his ears. A swift flutter made him jump into the protection of a breadfruit tree. But it was only a scarlet lory, startled off its perch. Something green spurted away from his path. An iguana.

A clearing opened ahead. Mahoney dropped to his knees and crawled forward, tired of breasting the jungle. Air plants drooped from the palms. Delicate orchids grew out of decayed bark.

Mahoney tugged at his sun helmet and eased the strap which had become soft with sweat. Trickles of moisture ran down inside his shirt, chilly against the heat of his body when they touched cloth.

"Perk up, my boy," muttered Mahoney. "You won't have to wait so long."

A bush moved in the soggy, motionless air. Another bush

shivered. A pair of eyes peered out, unblinking. A steel-shod arrow glittered briefly.

Mahoney jerked at his .45. His hand closed about the empty holster flap. Suddenly shaken, he grabbed for his rifle. Brown fingers clamped on the barrel. A spear jabbed his back.

For seconds nothing happened. The beads of perspiration gathered on Mahoney's brow and trickled off the end of his nose. The man across the clearing had not moved. A bee soared upward and broke the tension.

Inches at a time, Mahoney turned his head. A seamed, scowling face, daubed with white lines, was above him. Brittle eyes stared down at him. The man's arms folded across his withered, bare chest.

Mahoney knew without asking that this was the *orang kaya*—headman of the nearby village. The fantastic head jerked. Hands fastened upon Mahoney's shoulders and pulled him to his feet.

"You come along me," said the *orang kaya*. "Fellah boys got plenty surprise along you."

"Okay," replied Mahoney. "Lead off, aged patriarch."

The brown man walked sedately into the clearing. Men stood up on every side and closed in about Mahoney. They were very silent and their mouths were tight.

The procession went off at right angles to Mahoney's course. Men hacked at the confining, gripping underbrush with their trade machetes until they had reached the well-cleared pathway which led straight into the village.

Mahoney looked neither to right nor left. He knew nothing would earn him swifter annihilation than a show of fear.

Perhaps he could try to bluff them out of it, but then, when he asked himself how he would feel if he were chief and if some of his men had been bumped off . . .

The houses were built on stilts, flimsy structures of attap and crudely hewn logs. Pigs were tied to the posts and, at the appearance of the men, began to twist themselves up with the woven ropes, grunting.

Women, dressed in sarongs of trade calico, stole cautious glances through the thatch-rimmed windows. Children sat wide-mouthed in the yards and doors, solemnly studying this strangely quiet group.

The yards were well swept and free from grass. The brown earth was cracked open by the heat of the sun. The dead attap straggled out from the supporting beams.

At the far end of the village was a large clearing in the center of which stood a raised platform, evidently a seat of some kind. A huge flat rock lay before the platform. Mahoney did not miss the grooves which led down the sides. Those grooves were meant for blood.

On the platform five bodies were stretched, unlovely in the harsh light. The eyes stared unseeing at the metallic sky; the mouths gaped to display black tongues, and in each there was a jagged bullet hole.

Mahoney was ordered to halt before the high seat. He let his eyes rove the clearing. On stakes at regular intervals were curious things the size of baseballs. He went cold when he recognized them. Dried heads, left to appease the rather ferocious sun god, *Duadillah*.

The *orang kaya* sat down, folded his scrawny legs under him, clasped his scaly hands. Another man with a colorful headdress plunged out of the clearing edge and ran up to the chief's side.

Immediately there began a long, loud argument, attended by much hand-waving.

"Mahoney," said Mahoney, "I don't imagine that that is going to do you any good."

The *orang kaya* was apparently set on a particular idea. He kept pointing up at the staked heads. The other, obviously one of the *mana,* held out steadily, pointing continually to Mahoney.

Looking at the dried heads, Mahoney decided that he would not enjoy having his blind eyes stare out forever across this clearing with its grooved *Vatu Luli.*

The *noa* stood uneasily about, leaning upon their spears, trying to appear unconcerned. When the upper class talked, the lower class was never quite certain of the result.

Presently the *orang kaya* won out and glared down at Mahoney. "Hi, you. Look along stakes, huh?"

Mahoney had been looking along the stakes and the sight had been enough to last him for some time. Nevertheless, anxious for any pause, he carefully studied the row again.

Suddenly he felt as if a club had hit him in the face. One, two, three of those heads were topped by blond hair. White men! The clerks.

Mahoney tried to keep his voice level. "You kill them fellah boy?"

The *orang kaya* nodded benignly. "Now we kill you."

"You dry them three piece heads?"

Again the *orang kaya* nodded. Mahoney moved very cautiously, hoping that they would find nothing wrong in the move, until he could see the back of the first head. There had been something strange about the way the face bulged. He shuddered. The head had belonged to Harris, reported dead of fever.

Of course, the natives could have dug the body up, but Mahoney did not think so. He saw what he wanted to see then and stepped slowly and smoothly back before the platform.

The *orang kaya* slapped his hands together. Four of the *noas* leaped upon Mahoney. They pushed him down to his knees and began to tie his arms up behind him. Another came out of the jungle holding a bundle of sticks.

At least they looked like sticks. Then Mahoney saw that they were splinters, bamboo splinters, quite obviously poisoned.

Without waiting for any further orders, the man picked one out of the bundle and pointed it toward Mahoney's chest. Mahoney understood then. They'd make a porcupine out of him with those splinters and then the poison would swell him up like a blue balloon and he'd probably go mad before he died.

The *mana* with the headdress raised his voice stridently. It sounded like swearing to Mahoney. The man moved his arms at the sky and then at Mahoney.

The *orang kaya* sat up straight, scowling. He slapped his hands again and the bamboo was withdrawn. Mahoney was allowed to stand up once more.

"You," said the *orang kaya*, "plenty smart along gun."

Then Mahoney saw that they were splinters,
bamboo splinters, quite obviously poisoned.

"Certainly," agreed Mahoney.

"You plenty want to die all one piece or no die even though."

"Certainly," repeated Mahoney, his heart beginning to beat again.

"You shoot like I say, you go not dead."

"Anything you say," replied Mahoney. "Who do you want me to kill?"

"White man friend along you. The chief white man."

"You mean Anderson? Why do you want me to kill Anderson?"

"*Mana* here, he say fellah boy run trick along us. Fellah boy tell us lie. Fellah boy let us get five piece man dead."

Mahoney scowled. The *orang kaya* certainly had but little respect for Anderson, calling him fellah boy that way. But why should they want Anderson dead? Mahoney sidled around and looked at the back of Harris' dried head.

"All right," said Mahoney. "You come fast along me. We go make Anderson much dead."

The *mana* jerked his colored headgear and began to dance up and down in great excitement. A native ran out with the rifle and the .45 and thrust them into Mahoney's hands. The *noas* shouted and leaped about, expressing great joy, shaking their copper-tipped spears until the bamboo swooshed through the air.

They lost no time. With energy Mahoney had not suspected of them they launched themselves down the trail, running like so many panthers, very silent now that they had started.

Mahoney jogged along in their midst, wishing that the

heat would let up for a little while. Walking was bad enough. His head was filled with strange ideas, but he did not show on his face that he thought of anything.

After five minutes of this his lungs began to sizzle and curl up inside him. His boots gained a pound a step and his jerking rifle took on the feel of a howitzer. But the natives, under some stress he could not readily define, paid no attention whatever to the effects of this unaccustomed exercise.

The warehouse, a gray expanse writhing under heat waves, loomed through the thick tangle. The upper windows gaped emptily like the sightless eyes of the dried heads. The double door was barred securely.

The natives fell on their knees and crawled to the edge. They looked to their chief and the *mana* for instructions. The *mana* edged up beside Mahoney.

"You burn along that place, huh?" said the *mana*, black eyes glittering with excitement.

"It won't burn," replied Mahoney. "Godown tin, savvy? No burn."

"You burn along door."

Mahoney thought that over. Presently he extracted a cartridge from a clip and pulled the bullet out with his teeth. Tearing a piece off his shirttail, he poured half the powder into the cloth, folded it carefully. He thrust the end of the shell into the earth to pack it and then looked around for an arrow.

Taking the slender shaft, he impaled the cloth upon it.

Then he loaded the rifle with the blank and thrust the arrow down the barrel.

He aimed very carefully at the door, then fired. The powder-filled rag caught fire from the explosion. The arrow was shattered against the door, but the flame was there, licking steadily.

Evidently Anderson had not been aware of their presence. The gunshot brought a startled yelp from the interior. Feet pattered on the stairs and boards in the loft creaked.

Anderson stared out at the jungle edge and saw nothing.

"Shoot him," said the *mana*, urgently.

Mahoney shook his head. The *mana* promptly drew a short knife and shoved it against Mahoney's ribs. "Shoot!"

But Anderson had disappeared. He was instantly replaced by the black Melanesian faces of the imported soldiers. A rifle rapped sharply and the slug ripped through over Mahoney's head.

Working the bolt automatically, Mahoney fired before the echo of the first shot died. The black pitched out. He bounced as he hit and lay still.

"Anderson!" cried Mahoney. "Surrender to me!"

"The hell you say!"

The door was burning cheerfully now, its dry wood turning black all across the face. In a moment they would notice the smoke up there and try to put it out, but Mahoney knew that it was too late.

One door drifted open slowly, its bars burned through. Natives leaped to their feet and charged. Mahoney struggled up and ran after them. A rifle up in the window cracked. Mahoney stumbled. He caught a swift impression of a stubbly beard and squinted eyes.

"So much for you, you spy!" roared Anderson.

Mahoney struck the ground, carried forward by his own momentum. He kept rolling. In a second he was under the protection of the wall. A native dragged him inside. Something which wasn't sweat was running down under Mahoney's arm.

"Anderson," cried Mahoney, "if you surrender up there I'll see what I can do."

The natives swarmed through the deserted lower portion of the warehouse, unwilling to brave the stairs.

Anderson's voice came back. Mahoney thought it sounded a little tired. "Okay, Mahoney. I guess they got me. Come up."

Mahoney went to the stairs and started to ascend. He placed the rifle against the wall and took out his .45. His boots sounded hollow in the heavy tenseness which settled over the warehouse.

At the top of the steps, Mahoney paused. Anderson was standing in the middle of the floor, smiling. Mahoney stepped forward.

Suddenly two pairs of arms grabbed him. The .45 slid to the floor. Anderson held a bony finger to his lips for silence.

"One yelp," said Anderson, "and I'll plug you." He raised the pistol to firing position. The two soldiers who had stepped out from the wall behind the opening were grinning.

Mahoney snorted. "So what? You're trapped and you can't do a thing."

"I can kill you. I thought I did just now but I see I'm wrong.

So you got wise, did you? Thought I didn't know Murray sent you down here to find out what all this is about."

"Sure I knew," said Mahoney, putting up a front. "And I know you killed Harris. Shot him in the back of the head with that Navy pistol."

Anderson blinked.

"I saw his head at the village," continued Mahoney. "And I know now that you've been playing a pretty fast game with these natives here. You empty a warehouse of everything but a few trinkets. Then you excite these brown lads and get them to attack and kill the clerk so that your inventory will be safe.

"And then when the report is made up all the goods you took away from the place are reported lost. You sell these things yourself for your own profit."

"You're very clever, but not clever enough to save your own neck. I've still got influence with these fellows. They're just a little excited, that's all."

"Excited isn't any name for it. They got it doped out that you hired me to kill off a few of their men." Mahoney managed a smile. "They think in their simple way that the big boss white man has double-crossed them."

The pistol raised a little more. "You've got a letter of authority from Murray, haven't you?"

"Sure."

"And if I bump you off, he'll think things are crooked and follow you with another. Well, it ain't worrying me none, little boy. The fever got you like it got Harris. Turn around!"

"What's the matter? Can't you shoot a man when he's looking you in the eye?"

"Sure I can, Mahoney." The hammer came back with a loud click. The single-action revolver looked like a young cannon to Mahoney.

He heard a soft footfall on the steps. Mahoney smiled. "It won't be long, Anderson. You're burning up."

Anderson suddenly remembered the fire at the door. Inadvertently he looked toward the east window. The colored headdress of the *mana* came out of the stair opening like a jack-in-the-box.

Steel whistled through the air. The knife turned over once, twice. Anderson's eyes were suddenly staring at the headdress. The knife flickered and then did not flicker. The hilt protruded from Anderson's throat.

The Navy pistol thundered and then slammed to the planks. Anderson's body covered it up an instant later, bony hands contracting.

The blacks screamed and started for the opening, knocking Mahoney to one side. Mahoney snatched up the automatic as he dropped. He fired twice over the heads of the soldiers.

Faced by the staircase full of charging brown men, the blacks fell over themselves trying to get away from the trap. They huddled against the far wall, chattering in fear.

The *mana* gave the soldiers a disgusted look and then helped Mahoney to his feet. The natives clustered around, staring down at Anderson.

"Thanks," said Mahoney.

"White fellah boy," said the *mana*, "got too much power along here. Me, I be the witch doctor; he take my power. You, you got plenty power along you, but when he try to make us make you dead, I savvy him one piece devil. When you fight, I savvy you not know this fellah boy. You good fellah boy. Me, I good *mana*. You, me, make trade for people, keep people happy. *Orang kaya,* him like plenty fight. I not like plenty fight. Too much men get dead. Bad business *mana. Duadillah* not like."

"Okay," replied Mahoney, "okay." His eye caught a glitter beside the body of Anderson. It was the box of medals he had upset earlier in the day.

Mahoney scooped up a handful. He pinned one of them, a big brass one which said "First Prize Hog Calling," on the *mana's* sarong.

"That mean you plenty brave man," said Mahoney, very seriously.

"Plenty brave?" replied the *mana*. "Look."

The *mana* picked a whole handful off the floor and began to pin them across Mahoney's sweaty shirt front and although Mahoney's arm had begun to burn with wound fever, he smiled and looked down at the glittering, impressive row. Bicycle racing, broad jump, best steer, best pies and best—Mahoney couldn't believe his eyes—best marksmanship.

He took the last one off and pinned it on the *mana's* sarong. Very solemnly, they shook hands.

STORY PREVIEW

NOW that you've just ventured through some of the captivating tales in the Stories from the Golden Age collection by L. Ron Hubbard, turn the page and enjoy a preview of *Black Towers to Danger*. Join oil driller Murphy in the steamy jungles of Venezuela, where he finds himself the unwitting victim of a vicious plot to steal his land. Murder and double-dealing unfold when Murphy discovers that the woman he loves is in on the scheme, and he's forced to go head-to-head with an oil company that won't tolerate competition.

Black Towers to Danger

B ILL MURPHY had no premonition of danger when he turned down the slimy trail which wandered through the engulfing jungle above Lake Maracaibo.

He pulled up on his small horse, hooked the reins around the horn and wiped the sweat from his hands. Casually he began to build a cigarette.

He was not hurried about it. He had lots of time and he liked the flavor of his mission.

For two days Marcia Stewart had been at Camp Jaguar getting her late father's affairs in good order. It was time Bill Murphy made his call. He wondered if Marcia still thought that way about him. He hoped her dad wouldn't leave his ghost on the premises. Old man Stewart had been an oilman of the old hard school, a fighter to the last ditch. Now that he was gone, things ought to be fairly calm in Venezuela.

Unable to light a match, Bill removed his sunhat and ran the match through his hair to dry it. That done, he applied the flame to the cigarette.

The white helmet flew high and to the right.

The explosion came an instant later.

Bill Murphy had heard the shrill whine of the bullet.

Hastily he swung his mount into the shelter of a bush,

stepped off and hauled a Springfield from its boot. He went down into the muck on his hands and knees and crawled out for a better view.

A slug kicked splattering mud into his face.

"Damn," said Bill, unemotionally. He looked at his ruined white shirt and said "Damn," again.

He went around the other side of the bush, found himself still in shelter, crawled another ten feet and got a clear view of the enemy.

"Injun," said Bill.

He threw off the safety catch, sighted down the barrel through the number ten peep.

The Indian's black hair was glistening in a stray beam of sunlight. The cruel profile was set in a waiting expression.

Bill squeezed the trigger.

The Indian flipped backwards, his gun went up into the air and lit across his body.

Bill Murphy walked over to the clearing, leading his horse. He turned the body over with his foot.

"Camp Jaguar man," said Bill, in a disinterested fashion.

He sighed again and looked at his own muddy shirt which had so lately been stiff with starch for Marcia's benefit. Well, Marcia wouldn't love him the less for a dirty shirt if she loved him at all.

Bill swabbed the sweat from his forehead, inspected the hole in the sun helmet, replaced it. He mounted and headed down the twilight trail again with the flies buzzing around his head in pursuit formation.

"Dum de da de da," said Bill, thinking about Marcia again.

"Have to do something about these yellow devils," said Bill to his horse.

"Gettin' so it ain't safe to ride five miles from camp without having to waste ammunition on them. . . . Wonder if Marcia looks different."

He was drowsy with the heat and his great shoulders drooped forward a little. He was riding like a sack of meal when he came in sight of the oil derricks of Camp Jaguar.

The place hadn't changed much in the last two months. Old man Stewart was dead but the wells were still going down.

"Hello, Romano," said Bill. "Where's Marcia?"

Romano had been sitting on a rock with a rifle across his knees. He glanced angrily up at the machine-gun tower and saw that the guard was asleep.

Romano turned deliberately around. He hefted his rifle. His face was as thin as a dagger blade and his hair was very black. His skin had a yellow cast to it like an Indian's, but Romano claimed to be pure Castilian.

His eyes were squinted up.

"You better get the hell out of here, *amigo*," said Romano.

"What's the matter?" said Bill, rolling another cigarette and cocking a heel over the saddle.

"You know what's the matter," said Romano.

"Where's Marcia?"

Bill pulled a match from his sweat-stained pocket, rubbed it through his hair and lighted his smoke. He peered through the smoke haze at Romano.

"She don't want to see anything of you," said Romano, definitely.

"Let's see what Marcia says."

"You better get the hell out of here while you're all whole," said Romano.

Bill put his boot back in the stirrup and glanced up toward the shack he knew Marcia would occupy. He sighed, took another drag on the tattered cigarette and started to move off.

Romano leaped into the trail ahead of him, rifle leveled.

"I'm going to shoot," cried Romano.

Bill leaned over and grabbed the barrel. He canted the rifle and pulled it to him. Romano had to let go or get a broken wrist. Bill jacked the shells out of the magazine and put them into his pocket.

Romano yelled for help and tried to get at his revolver. Bill leaned over and took that and threw it into the brush. With a sharp crack, the rifle butt connected with the seat of Romano's pants.

Bill threw the rifle after the revolver and rode easily up toward the shack.

He got down and walked up the steps. He knocked.

Marcia threw back the door and turned white. She looked hard at Bill and then her eyes began to kindle. Her voice sounded as if words were about to stick in her throat and choke her.

"What do you mean by coming here?" said Marcia, angry.

"Oh, I just thought I'd mosey up and see if you were settled yet," said Bill.

"You two-faced, sneaking thief! You . . . you murderer!"

"Well, now," said Bill defensively. "I wouldn't go as far as that. Of course I might have shot Pedro, but . . . "

"Pedro! Another one! First it was Miguel and then Dad and now Pedro. Romano! Romano! Get the men!"

Bill looked at her. He took out a wet handkerchief and mopped at his face. He put it back in his pocket and looked down the trail.

Romano was trying to find the revolver in the brush.

"Get out!" said Marcia, pointing, her mouth set.

Bill looked her over. Yes, he had been right. She was prettier than ever. She was nice and slim and right now she was dressed in a riding skirt and a man's white shirt with rolled-up sleeves. Her brown hair was curly and crisp and feminine. Her face was a perfect oval and her mouth, when she wanted it to be, was kind.

But she could get mad.

To find out more about *Black Towers to Danger* and how you can obtain your copy, go to www.goldenagestories.com.

GLOSSARY

STORIES FROM THE GOLDEN AGE *reflect the words and expressions used in the 1930s and 1940s, adding unique flavor and authenticity to the tales. While a character's speech may often reflect regional origins, it also can convey attitudes common in the day. So that readers can better grasp such cultural and historical terms, uncommon words or expressions of the era, the following glossary has been provided.*

---

accouterments: pieces of military equipment carried by soldiers in addition to their standard uniform and weapons.

Ahaggar Plateau: a highland region in the central Sahara, located in southern Algeria. It is an arid, rocky upland region and the home of the formerly nomadic Tuareg.

aileron: a hinged flap on the trailing edge of an aircraft wing, used to control banking movements.

Alexandria: the second largest city in Egypt and its largest seaport, extending about twenty miles along the coast of the Mediterranean Sea in north central Egypt.

attap: a type of palm, the fronds of which are used in the making of buildings.

Berbers: members of a people living in North Africa, primarily Muslim, living in settled or nomadic tribes between the Sahara and Mediterranean Sea and between Egypt and the Atlantic Ocean.

boot: saddle boot; a close-fitting covering or case for a gun or other weapon that straps to a saddle.

bowsprit: a spar projecting from the upper end of the bow of a sailing vessel, for holding and supporting a sail.

club: airplane propeller.

djellaba: a long loose hooded garment with full sleeves, worn especially in Muslim countries.

ducks: slacks or trousers; pants made of a heavy, plain-weave cotton fabric.

Fijis: the Fiji Islands, a South Pacific nation comprised of 322 islands. About 100 are inhabited, while the balance remain nature preserves. They were once known as the Cannibal Isles because of the ferocious natives. The majority of the Fiji Islands are mountainous (volcanic in origin), with several peaks exceeding 3,000 feet. The balance of the smaller islands are a mixture of coral and limestone. In 1874 Fiji became a British colony, and gained its independence in 1970, after nearly a century of British control.

flimflam: to trick, deceive, swindle or cheat.

forty-five or **.45:** a handgun chambered to fire a .45-caliber cartridge.

G-men: government men; agents of the Federal Bureau of Investigation.

godown: a warehouse; a commercial building for storage of goods.

ground loop: to cause an aircraft to ground loop, or make a sharp horizontal turn when taxiing, landing or taking off.

hard-boiled: tough; unsentimental.

howitzer: a cannon which has a comparatively short barrel, used especially for firing shells at a high angle of elevation for a short range, as for reaching a target behind cover or in a trench.

ifrīt: (Arabic) a powerful evil *jinn*, demon or monstrous giant in Arabic mythology.

imajeghen: (Tamasheq) the Tuareg noble class.

imghad: (Tamasheq) the Tuareg vassal class that serves the nobles.

jinnī or *jinn:* (Arabic) *jinnī* singular, *jinn* plural; in Muslim legend, a spirit often capable of assuming human or animal form and exercising supernatural influence over people.

keel: a lengthwise structure along the base of a ship, and in some vessels extended downwards as a ridge to increase stability.

Lake Maracaibo: an inlet of the Caribbean Sea in northwestern Venezuela. The largest natural lake in South America, it occupies an area of 5,130 square miles.

Liberia: a country on the west coast of Africa, bordered by Sierra Leone, Guinea and Côte d'Ivoire. Liberia, which means "Land of the Free," was founded as an independent nation with support of the American government, for free-born and formerly enslaved African-Americans.

lugger: an old, slow cargo vessel.

Malay: the race of people who inhabit the Malay Peninsula and portions of adjacent islands of southeast Asia.

mameluke: (Arabic) a member of a military caste, originally made up of slaves, that ruled in Egypt from 1250 until 1517 and remained powerful until 1811.

mana: (Polynesian) one with power; an authority.

Marianas: Mariana Islands; a group of fifteen islands in the western Pacific Ocean, about three-quarters of the way from Hawaii to the Philippines. It consists of two groups: a northern group of ten volcanic main islands, of which only four (Agrihan, Anatahan, Alamagan and Pagan) are inhabited; and a southern group of five islands (Rota, Guam, Aguijan, Tinian and Saipan), of which all are inhabited save Aguijan.

marid: a *jinnī* of the most powerful class, gigantic in size.

Melanesian: a member of a people native to a division of Oceania in the southwest Pacific Ocean, comprising the islands northeast of Australia and south of the equator. It includes the Solomon Islands. The Melanesian people primarily fish and farm, and supplement their economy by exporting cacao, copra (coconut) and copper.

muezzin: a man who calls Muslims to prayer from the minaret (a slender tower with a balcony) of a mosque.

noa: (Polyneasian) common people; a Polynesian term used in place of the actual name of someone.

orang kaya: headman; before the arrival of Europeans, the

people of Banda had a form of government led by *orang kaya* (powerful men).

Papuans: a member of any of the indigenous people of New Guinea and neighboring islands.

petcock: a small valve used to control the flow of gas.

pink tea: formal tea, reception or other social gathering usually attended by politicians, military officials and the like.

pipe-clayed: clean and smart; pipe clay is a fine white clay used in whitening leather. It was at one time largely used by soldiers for making their gloves, accouterments and clothes look clean and smart.

Polynesian: a native or inhabitant of Polynesia, a large grouping of over 1,000 islands scattered over the central and southern Pacific Ocean.

quirt: a riding whip with a short handle and a braided leather lash.

Salonika: also Thessaloniki; city and port located in northeastern Greece. It is the second largest city and the capital of the Greek region of Macedonia.

Savile Row: a street in Great Britain renowned for exquisite custom tailoring of men's clothing.

saw-grass: grass named because the edges of the leaves are notched like a saw with teeth.

Scheherazade: the female narrator of *The Arabian Nights*, who during one thousand and one adventurous nights saved her life by entertaining her husband, the king, with stories.

schooner: a fast sailing ship with at least two masts and with sails set lengthwise.

scimitar: a curved, single-edged sword of Oriental origin.

seal of Solomon: a magical signet ring said to have been possessed by King Solomon, a wise ruler of an empire centered on the United Kingdom of Israel, which gave him the power to command demons (or *jinn*), or to speak with animals. The signet consists of two equilateral triangles, interlaced so as to form a star, and surrounded by a circle. This symbol is thought to have the power to drive away demons.

Shanghai: city of eastern China at the mouth of the Yangtze River, and the largest city in the country. Shanghai was opened to foreign trade by treaty in 1842 and quickly prospered. France, Great Britain and the United States all held large concessions (rights to use land granted by a government) in the city until the early twentieth century.

slipstream: the airstream pushed back by a revolving aircraft propeller.

Societies: Society Islands; an island group within French Polynesia in the South Pacific, originally claimed in 1843. Considered "Paradise on Earth," they were explored by Captains Cook and Bligh. Divided into the Windward Islands and the Leeward Islands, they were given their name by Captain James Cook in 1769, when he named them after England's Royal Society. Most of these rugged islands are volcanic in origin, with a few small coral atolls mixed in. Of these, the most recognizable names are the legendary islands of Bora Bora, Huahine, Moorea and Tahiti.

Solomons: Solomon Islands; a group of islands northeast of Australia. They form a double chain of six large islands, about twenty medium-sized ones and numerous smaller islets and reefs.

Southern Cross: four bright stars in the southern hemisphere that are situated as if to form a cross and used for navigation.

Springfield: any of several types of rifle, named after Springfield, Massachusetts, the site of a federal armory that made the rifles.

Sudanese: people of Sudan, the largest country in Africa, bordered by Egypt to the north and the Red Sea to the northeast.

Tamasheq: a Berber language spoken by the Tuareg.

Tārgi: (Arabic) inhabitant of Targa, the Tuareg name of a southwestern desert region and a former province of Libya.

tender: a small boat used to ferry passengers and light cargo between ship and shore.

trepang: a sea cucumber of the southern Pacific and Indian oceans, dried or smoked for use as an ingredient in soup.

Tuaregs: members of the nomadic Berber-speaking people of the southwestern Sahara in Africa. They have traditionally engaged in herding, agriculture and convoying caravans across their territories. The Tuaregs became among the most hostile of all the colonized peoples of French West Africa, because they were among the most affected by colonial policies. In 1917, they fought a vicious and bloody war against the French, but they were defeated and as a result, dispossessed of traditional grazing lands. They are known to be fierce warriors; European explorers expressed their fear by warning, "The scorpion and the Tuareg are the only enemies you meet in the desert."

Vatu Luli: a sacrificial stone.

windage: the amount of adjustment needed in the aiming of a projectile to counter wind deflection.

wingover: also known as the Immelmann turn; an aerial maneuver named after World War I flying ace Max Immelmann. The pilot pulls the aircraft into a vertical climb, applying full rudder as the speed drops, then rolls the aircraft while pulling back slightly on the stick, causing the aircraft to dive back down in the opposite direction. It has become one of the most popular aerial maneuvers in the world.

witch doctor: a person who is believed to heal through magical powers.

yawl: a sailing vessel rigged fore and aft with a large mainmast and a smaller mizzenmast (the third mast on a vessel having three or more masts) toward the stern.

L. Ron Hubbard
in the Golden Age
of Pulp Fiction

*In writing an adventure story
a writer has to know that he is adventuring
for a lot of people who cannot.
The writer has to take them here and there
about the globe and show them
excitement and love and realism.
As long as that writer is living the part of an
adventurer when he is hammering
the keys, he is succeeding with his story.*

*Adventuring is a state of mind.
If you adventure through life, you have a
good chance to be a success on paper.*

*Adventure doesn't mean globe-trotting,
exactly, and it doesn't mean great deeds.
Adventuring is like art.
You have to live it to make it real.*

— *L. Ron Hubbard*

L. Ron Hubbard
and American
Pulp Fiction

B ORN March 13, 1911, L. Ron Hubbard lived a life at least as expansive as the stories with which he enthralled a hundred million readers through a fifty-year career.

Originally hailing from Tilden, Nebraska, he spent his formative years in a classically rugged Montana, replete with the cowpunchers, lawmen and desperadoes who would later people his Wild West adventures. And lest anyone imagine those adventures were drawn from vicarious experience, he was not only breaking broncs at a tender age, he was also among the few whites ever admitted into Blackfoot society as a bona fide blood brother. While if only to round out an otherwise rough and tumble youth, his mother was that rarity of her time—a thoroughly educated woman—who introduced her son to the classics of Occidental literature even before his seventh birthday.

But as any dedicated L. Ron Hubbard reader will attest, his world extended far beyond Montana. In point of fact, and as the son of a United States naval officer, by the age of eighteen he had traveled over a quarter of a million miles. Included therein were three Pacific crossings to a then still mysterious Asia, where he ran with the likes of Her British Majesty's agent-in-place

L. Ron Hubbard, left, at Congressional Airport, Washington, DC, 1931, with members of George Washington University flying club.

for North China, and the last in the line of Royal Magicians from the court of Kublai Khan. For the record, L. Ron Hubbard was also among the first Westerners to gain admittance to forbidden Tibetan monasteries below Manchuria, and his photographs of China's Great Wall long graced American geography texts.

Upon his return to the United States and a hasty completion of his interrupted high school education, the young Ron Hubbard entered George Washington University. There, as fans of his aerial adventures may have heard, he earned his wings as a pioneering barnstormer at the dawn of American aviation. He also earned a place in free-flight record books for the longest sustained flight above Chicago. Moreover, as a roving reporter for *Sportsman Pilot* (featuring his first professionally penned articles), he further helped inspire a generation of pilots who would take America to world airpower.

Immediately beyond his sophomore year, Ron embarked on the first of his famed ethnological expeditions, initially to then untrammeled Caribbean shores (descriptions of which would later fill a whole series of West Indies mystery-thrillers). That the Puerto Rican interior would also figure into the future of Ron Hubbard stories was likewise no accident. For in addition to cultural studies of the island, a 1932–33

LRH expedition is rightly remembered as conducting the first complete mineralogical survey of a Puerto Rico under United States jurisdiction.

There was many another adventure along this vein: As a lifetime member of the famed Explorers Club, L. Ron Hubbard charted North Pacific waters with the first shipboard radio direction finder, and so pioneered a long-range navigation system universally employed until the late twentieth century. While not to put too fine an edge on it, he also held a rare Master Mariner's license to pilot any vessel, of any tonnage in any ocean.

Yet lest we stray too far afield, there is an LRH note at this juncture in his saga, and it reads in part:

"I started out writing for the pulps, writing the best I knew, writing for every mag on the stands, slanting as well as I could."

To which one might add: His earliest submissions date from the summer of 1934, and included tales drawn from true-to-life Asian adventures, with characters roughly modeled on British/American intelligence operatives he had known in Shanghai. His early Westerns were similarly peppered with details drawn from personal experience. Although therein lay a first hard lesson from the often cruel world of the pulps. His first Westerns were soundly rejected as lacking the authenticity of a Max Brand yarn

Capt. L. Ron Hubbard in Ketchikan, Alaska, 1940, on his Alaskan Radio Experimental Expedition, the first of three voyages conducted under the Explorers Club flag.

(a particularly frustrating comment given L. Ron Hubbard's Westerns came straight from his Montana homeland, while Max Brand was a mediocre New York poet named Frederick Schiller Faust, who turned out implausible six-shooter tales from the terrace of an Italian villa).

Nevertheless, and needless to say, L. Ron Hubbard persevered and soon earned a reputation as among the most publishable names in pulp fiction, with a ninety percent placement rate of first-draft manuscripts. He was also among the most prolific, averaging between seventy and a hundred thousand words a month. Hence the rumors that L. Ron Hubbard had redesigned a typewriter for faster keyboard action and pounded out manuscripts on a continuous roll of butcher paper to save the precious seconds it took to insert a single sheet of paper into manual typewriters of the day.

That all L. Ron Hubbard stories did not run beneath said byline is yet another aspect of pulp fiction lore. That is, as publishers periodically rejected manuscripts from top-drawer authors if only to avoid paying top dollar, L. Ron Hubbard and company just as frequently replied with submissions under various pseudonyms. In Ron's case, the list

A MAN OF MANY NAMES

Between 1934 and 1950, L. Ron Hubbard authored more than fifteen million words of fiction in more than two hundred classic publications. To supply his fans and editors with stories across an array of genres and pulp titles, he adopted fifteen pseudonyms in addition to his already renowned L. Ron Hubbard byline.

Winchester Remington Colt
Lt. Jonathan Daly
Capt. Charles Gordon
Capt. L. Ron Hubbard
Bernard Hubbel
Michael Keith
Rene Lafayette
Legionnaire 148
Legionnaire 14830
Ken Martin
Scott Morgan
Lt. Scott Morgan
Kurt von Rachen
Barry Randolph
Capt. Humbert Reynolds

126

included: Rene Lafayette, Captain Charles Gordon, Lt. Scott Morgan and the notorious Kurt von Rachen—supposedly on the lam for a murder rap, while hammering out two-fisted prose in Argentina. The point: While L. Ron Hubbard as Ken Martin spun stories of Southeast Asian intrigue, LRH as Barry Randolph authored tales of

L. Ron Hubbard, circa 1930, at the outset of a literary career that would finally span half a century.

romance on the Western range—which, stretching between a dozen genres is how he came to stand among the two hundred elite authors providing close to a million tales through the glory days of American Pulp Fiction.

In evidence of exactly that, by 1936 L. Ron Hubbard was literally leading pulp fiction's elite as president of New York's American Fiction Guild. Members included a veritable pulp hall of fame: Lester "Doc Savage" Dent, Walter "The Shadow" Gibson, and the legendary Dashiell Hammett—to cite but a few.

Also in evidence of just where L. Ron Hubbard stood within his first two years on the American pulp circuit: By the spring of 1937, he was ensconced in Hollywood, adopting a Caribbean thriller for Columbia Pictures, remembered today as *The Secret of Treasure Island.* Comprising fifteen thirty-minute episodes, the L. Ron Hubbard screenplay led to the most profitable matinée serial in Hollywood history. In accord with Hollywood culture, he was thereafter continually called

The 1937 Secret of Treasure Island, *a fifteen-episode serial adapted for the screen by L. Ron Hubbard from his novel,* Murder at Pirate Castle.

upon to rewrite/doctor scripts—most famously for long-time friend and fellow adventurer Clark Gable.

In the interim—and herein lies another distinctive chapter of the L. Ron Hubbard story—he continually worked to open Pulp Kingdom gates to up-and-coming authors. Or, for that matter, anyone who wished to write. It was a fairly unconventional stance, as markets were already thin and competition razor sharp. But the fact remains, it was an L. Ron Hubbard hallmark that he vehemently lobbied on behalf of young authors—regularly supplying instructional articles to trade journals, guest-lecturing to short story classes at George Washington University and Harvard, and even founding his own creative writing competition. It was established in 1940, dubbed the Golden Pen, and guaranteed winners both New York representation and publication in *Argosy.*

But it was John W. Campbell Jr.'s *Astounding Science Fiction* that finally proved the most memorable LRH vehicle. While every fan of L. Ron Hubbard's galactic epics undoubtedly knows the story, it nonetheless bears repeating: By late 1938, the pulp publishing magnate of Street & Smith was determined to revamp *Astounding Science Fiction* for broader readership. In particular, senior editorial director F. Orlin Tremaine called for stories with a stronger *human element.* When acting editor John W. Campbell balked, preferring his spaceship-driven tales,

Tremaine enlisted Hubbard. Hubbard, in turn, replied with the genre's first truly *character-driven* works, wherein heroes are pitted not against bug-eyed monsters but the mystery and majesty of deep space itself—and thus was launched the Golden Age of Science Fiction.

The names alone are enough to quicken the pulse of any science fiction aficionado, including LRH friend and protégé, Robert Heinlein, Isaac Asimov, A. E. van Vogt and Ray Bradbury. Moreover, when coupled with LRH stories of fantasy, we further come to what's rightly been described as the foundation of every modern tale of horror: L. Ron Hubbard's immortal *Fear*. It was rightly proclaimed by Stephen King as one of the very few works to genuinely warrant that overworked term "classic"—as in: *"This is a classic tale of creeping, surreal menace and horror. . . . This is one of the really, really good ones."*

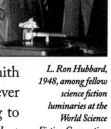

L. Ron Hubbard, 1948, among fellow science fiction luminaries at the World Science Fiction Convention in Toronto.

To accommodate the greater body of L. Ron Hubbard fantasies, Street & Smith inaugurated *Unknown*—a classic pulp if there ever was one, and wherein readers were soon thrilling to the likes of *Typewriter in the Sky* and *Slaves of Sleep* of which Frederik Pohl would declare: *"There are bits and pieces from Ron's work that became part of the language in ways that very few other writers managed."*

And, indeed, at J. W. Campbell Jr.'s insistence, Ron was regularly drawing on themes from the Arabian Nights and

129

so introducing readers to a world of genies, jinn, Aladdin and Sinbad—all of which, of course, continue to float through cultural mythology to this day.

At least as influential in terms of post-apocalypse stories was L. Ron Hubbard's 1940 *Final Blackout*. Generally acclaimed as the finest anti-war novel of the decade and among the ten best works of the genre ever authored—here, too, was a tale that would live on in ways few other writers

imagined. Hence, the later Robert Heinlein verdict: "Final Blackout *is as perfect a piece of science fiction as has ever been written.*"

Like many another who both lived and wrote American pulp adventure, the war proved a tragic end to Ron's sojourn in the pulps. He served with distinction in four theaters and was highly decorated

Portland, Oregon, 1943; L. Ron Hubbard captain of the US Navy subchaser PC 815.

for commanding corvettes in the North Pacific. He was also grievously wounded in combat, lost many a close friend and colleague and thus resolved to say farewell to pulp fiction and devote himself to what it had supported these many years—namely, his serious research.

But in no way was the LRH literary saga at an end, for as he wrote some thirty years later, in 1980:

"Recently there came a period when I had little to do. This was novel in a life so crammed with busy years, and I decided to amuse myself by writing a novel that was pure science fiction."

That work was *Battlefield Earth: A Saga of the Year 3000*. It was an immediate *New York Times* bestseller and, in fact, the first international science fiction blockbuster in decades. It was not, however, L. Ron Hubbard's magnum opus, as that distinction is generally reserved for his next and final work: The 1.2 million word *Mission Earth*.

> **Final Blackout**
> *is as perfect*
> *a piece of*
> *science fiction as*
> *has ever*
> *been written.*
>
> —Robert Heinlein

How he managed those 1.2 million words in just over twelve months is yet another piece of the L. Ron Hubbard legend. But the fact remains, he did indeed author a ten-volume *dekalogy* that lives in publishing history for the fact that each and every volume of the series was also a *New York Times* bestseller.

Moreover, as subsequent generations discovered L. Ron Hubbard through republished works and novelizations of his screenplays, the mere fact of his name on a cover signaled an international bestseller. . . . Until, to date, sales of his works exceed hundreds of millions, and he otherwise remains among the most enduring and widely read authors in literary history. Although as a final word on the tales of L. Ron Hubbard, perhaps it's enough to simply reiterate what editors told readers in the glory days of American Pulp Fiction:

He writes the way he does, brothers, because he's been there, seen it and done it!

THE STORIES FROM THE
GOLDEN AGE

Your ticket to adventure starts here with the Stories from
the Golden Age collection by master storyteller L. Ron Hubbard.
These gripping tales are set in a kaleidoscope of exotic locales and brim
with fascinating characters, including some of the
most vile villains, dangerous dames and brazen heroes
you'll ever get to meet.

The entire collection of over one hundred and fifty stories is being
released in a series of eighty books and audiobooks.
For an up-to-date listing of available titles,
go to www.goldenagestories.com.

AIR ADVENTURE

Arctic Wings	*Man-Killers of the Air*
The Battling Pilot	*On Blazing Wings*
Boomerang Bomber	*Red Death Over China*
The Crate Killer	*Sabotage in the Sky*
The Dive Bomber	*Sky Birds Dare!*
Forbidden Gold	*The Sky-Crasher*
Hurtling Wings	*Trouble on His Wings*
The Lieutenant Takes the Sky	*Wings Over Ethiopia*

FAR-FLUNG ADVENTURE

SEA ADVENTURE

TALES FROM THE ORIENT

MYSTERY

FANTASY

SCIENCE FICTION

WESTERN

The Baron of Coyote River	*Man for Breakfast*
Blood on His Spurs	*The No-Gun Gunhawk*
Boss of the Lazy B	*The No-Gun Man*
Branded Outlaw	*The Ranch That No One Would Buy*
Cattle King for a Day	*Reign of the Gila Monster*
Come and Get It	*Ride 'Em, Cowboy*
Death Waits at Sundown	*Ruin at Rio Piedras*
Devil's Manhunt	*Shadows from Boot Hill*
The Ghost Town Gun-Ghost	*Silent Pards*
Gun Boss of Tumbleweed	*Six-Gun Caballero*
Gunman!	*Stacked Bullets*
Gunman's Tally	*Stranger in Town*
The Gunner from Gehenna	*Tinhorn's Daughter*
Hoss Tamer	*The Toughest Ranger*
Johnny, the Town Tamer	*Under the Diehard Brand*
King of the Gunmen	*Vengeance Is Mine!*
The Magic Quirt	*When Gilhooly Was in Flower*

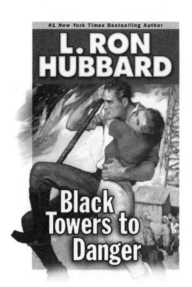

JOIN THE PULP REVIVAL
America in the 1930s and 40s

Pulp fiction was in its heyday and 30 million readers were regularly riveted by the larger-than-life tales of master storyteller L. Ron Hubbard. For this was pulp fiction's golden age, when the writing was raw and every page packed a walloping punch.

That magic can now be yours. An evocative world of nefarious villains, exotic intrigues, courageous heroes and heroines—a world that today's cinema has barely tapped for tales of adventure and swashbucklers.

Enroll today in the Stories from the Golden Age Club and begin receiving your monthly feature edition selected from more than 150 stories in the collection.

You may choose to enjoy them as either a paperback or audiobook for the special membership price of $9.95 each month along with FREE shipping and handling.

CALL TOLL-FREE: 1-877-8GALAXY
(1-877-842-5299) OR GO ONLINE TO
www.goldenagestories.com
AND BECOME PART OF THE PULP REVIVAL!

Prices are set in US dollars only. For non-US residents, please call
1-323-466-7815 for pricing information. Free shipping available for US residents only.

Galaxy Press, 7051 Hollywood Blvd., Suite 200, Hollywood, CA 90028